The
# Ten-Day
# Daughter

*The*
# TEN-DAY
# Daughter

## S. MICHAEL WILCOX

EAGLE
GATE

SALT LAKE CITY, UTAH

*To Our Ten-Day Daughter,*
*Wherever She May Be.*

Visit us at EagleGate.com

---

**Library of Congress Cataloging-in-Publication Data**

(CIP information on file)

ISBN 978-1-60907-204-9

---

Printed in the United States of America
Alexander's Print Advantage, Lindon, UT

10   9   8   7   6   5   4   3   2   1

*And it came to pass*
*That the Lord spake unto Enoch,*
*And told Enoch*
*All the doings*
*Of the children of men;*

*Wherefore Enoch knew,*
*And looked*
*Upon their wickedness,*
*And their misery,*
*And wept*

*And stretched forth his arms,*
*And his heart swelled*
*Wide as eternity;*
*And his bowels yearned;*
*And all eternity shook.*

—MOSES 7:41

# Contents

# Preface

The following story was destined to be fiction; not because I wanted to write a fiction, but because I could not write it the way it really happened. I tried. There were too many unanswered questions. I had crossed a frontier into a country, the language of which I had but a dim recollection.

So I wrote a catharsis, one I could live with. The writing helped to shift my memories to new areas where they could be endured; because I cannot yet speak that language.

S. M. W.

# Chapter 1

*I*n the melting pot of America, Boulder, Colorado, has stubbornly—almost proudly—refused to melt. Every spring Boulder sends the mystery of a migratory summons down the lines of the nation's highways, and the wandering, discontented, searching—often tragically tormented—thousands respond. They come to meet and live out a tiny particle of life. Then they are gone.

In the center of Boulder is the University of Colorado. The campus is immersed in the rich, clean green of living things, its buildings shaded by the Rocky Mountains. A green ivy covers the almond sandstone, but in autumn the leaves turn blood-red before drifting to the ground, to be stirred into neglected corners by the ceaseless passing of student feet.

If those walking feet cross the street at an angle from the student center, they will come to the LDS Institute of Religion. And it is here, for the past few years, I have inherited the often delicate responsibility of dealing with the human driftwood that comes with each spring's runoff. Flowing into Boulder, they spread out onto the Pearl Street Mall, where on any given day one can meet every variation humanity has to offer. Often, that humanity reaches across the green island of the university to settle into the institute's lounge. On occasion, two or three a week will shuffle into the institute with their overstuffed backpacks. With a weary sigh they will ask for money or a meal, or if they could just sleep on the couches. I have learned to keep a little money in the cash box to pay for a few hours' work, which they are usually willing to contribute to the grounds or building. More often they just want to talk.

During this season two years ago, while working at home, I received a phone call from my secretary. She had been baptized into the Church three months before and had been with me for less than two weeks. Not much taller than 5'4", with a distinctive thinness, she made up for her lack of physical stature by an overabundant eagerness in her personality and in her flair for western clothes and music. I always thought it a unique combination. It took me three days to convince her that the proper attire for an institute secretary was a dress, not designer jeans and cowboy boots. She was the perfect institute secretary, however: friendly to the point of boldness, caring, efficient, incurably optimistic about her new faith, and unafraid to tell me when I was wrong.

"Brother Christianson," she said somewhat urgently, "I think you need to come up to the institute."

My home was in a little community fifteen miles down the freeway from Boulder. I was covered with mud from a vain attempt to chisel garden seeds into the granite clay of my backyard. I replied: "Karen, I'm filthy from my garden. I can't come up now. Can't you handle it?"

"I'm trying, but she wants to leave and she shouldn't. She wants to talk to the reverend."

Her voice was hurried, near a whisper, troubled with frustration. I said to myself, *Remember, this is her nature.*

"What reverend, Karen? I can hardly hear you. Are you whispering on purpose?"

"She doesn't like loud voices. Please, Brother Christianson, I need you to come."

"Who's 'she'? What are you talking about? I'm not a reverend, Karen—I'm just the institute director. Don't you mean the bishop? Didn't the elders explain about bishops? We don't have reverends in our church."

"No! You don't understand."

"Karen, can you talk a little louder? The kids are being noisy."

"I can't. It scares her."

"What *her?* Who's with you?"

"She won't tell me her name. She says she wants to talk to the reverend."

"Bishop," I corrected. She ignored me and continued.

"She's going to leave. She's pregnant and doesn't look good."

"Is she from Pearl Street?"

"I think so. She says she'll only talk to the reverend."

"I'm not a reverend, Karen."

"She thinks you are. You're the one she wants to see. Will you come?"

"I'm covered in mud."

"He told her you'd help her."

"*Who* told her?"

"Someone at the mall."

"Does she need money? The cash box . . ."

"She's pregnant. I can't make her work. She just wants to talk to you. She won't talk to me, and she gets up to leave every few minutes because she's afraid. I really shouldn't have talked to you this long."

"Are you sure she really wants to talk to me? Maybe you should just let her leave."

"No. She's not like the others—she's different."

"Maybe she's in trouble."

"If you see her, you'll want to talk to her."

"All right, Karen. I'll come as quickly as I can."

"Could you put on your blue suit and a white shirt so you'd look a little like a reverend? I think you might scare her with muddy clothes on."

I hung up the phone, thoroughly bewildered, as my wife came into the kitchen.

"Who was that?"

"Karen. We have another transient at the institute. A girl. She wants to talk to 'the reverend.'"

"Who?"

"I'm not sure, but I guess I'm going to have to drive up to Boulder."

"It's that urgent? I don't think the kids will wait for dinner."

"Karen sounded pretty desperate. She's a new convert; for her sake I'd better go up and at least make an appearance."

I showered, put on a white shirt and a dark blue suit, and drove up to Boulder. It was dark when I arrived. I parked my car in my usual space by the west door. From there I could see into the building, down the hall, past the kitchen, my office, and into the lounge. There was only a small lamp on. That puzzled me because we always left the hall lights on for security.

Karen must have been sitting in the semi-dark lounge watching the west doorway because she tiptoed to the door, came out, and put her finger to her lips as I closed my car door.

"Why are the hall lights off, Karen?"

"She's sleeping. She was exhausted. She probably walked around the mall all day. I don't think she'll wake up till morning."

"I thought you could hardly keep her from leaving."

"When I told her you were coming, she sat down on the couch and started to relax. In the middle of a sentence she fell asleep. I'm sorry you came up for nothing. I guess I panicked again."

"Karen, she can't sleep in the institute."

"I'll stay with her."

"You can't sleep in the institute either. It's policy. There are other places we can take her, to a member's home if we have to. The Church has a division called LDS Social Services who handle things like this. This is the institute. I can't have her sleep here even if you stay."

"Can't you come and see her? She can't be much older than eighteen or nineteen. I'd take her home if I thought she'd come with me, but she's afraid of everything. Every car that passes makes her jump. Maybe I should have taken her to the couch upstairs, but she wanted to be near the door."

"Maybe she's done something wrong. We've had all kinds come off the mall."

"Come and see her first. She hasn't done anything wrong. She's just afraid."

"All right. Let's go look at her."

"Don't wake her up. I'm afraid if she woke up and saw you standing over her, she'd go to pieces."

I entered the institute like a thief, removing my shoes as I walked up the linoleum hallway. Once in the lounge I moved quietly to the couch and stood behind it so if she did wake up she wouldn't see me. As I stared down in the dim light of the single lamp, I saw a girl lying sideways on the couch, deep in sleep. Her lips, partially opened, pulled a troubled breath with labor into her lungs. She was barely five feet tall and if she hadn't been pregnant would have weighed under a hundred pounds. Recalling the births of my own children, it was apparent she was in the last few weeks of her pregnancy. Even curled up as she was I could tell the baby had dropped. I gazed at her face which had a certain elfin quality, fine, delicate, and slightly pinched.

Her blonde hair was pulled tightly into a bun that now had wisps of hair falling out on every side, lying lightly in quiet disarray against her face. Even in the yellow lamplight her skin was white, almost translucent. I wondered many times in the days that followed if any amount of sunlight could ever tan that paleness from her features. Her thin fingers were curled tightly around the cloth handles of the bag she carried. Her clothes were clean but wrinkled as if they had been pulled directly from the washing machine. They were the color of spring—yellows and light blues—and she wore white tennis shoes. The cloth bag which she gripped so tightly was large enough to hold a small typewriter. It appeared to be stuffed with extra clothes. Later we found out it also contained some art supplies, a journal of some kind, and a little cheese and bread. There was a Dickensian child-like innocence about her which produced sympathy for her immediately in my heart.

"Have you found out her name?" I whispered to Karen.

"No—she wouldn't tell me."

"You know I can't stay here with you, Karen. If you need any help, I'm twenty minutes away."

"She doesn't look like she could hurt anyone."

"No, I guess not."

"So I'll be fine."

"Okay, I'll be back at six. I'll bring up some eggs and juice for breakfast. If you need any help, call."

I drove home wondering what it was about this wanderer that touched me so deeply. I was concerned about her and Karen sleeping in the building but felt this was one exception I could live with.

At six the next morning I was back at the institute with the food that I had promised. Karen met me at the west door.

"She went back to sleep again."

"She woke up?"

"On and off throughout the night. She would yell strange things in her sleep, pleading with somebody, saying 'Stop, stop!' over and over again. Then she'd wake up afraid and try to run until she knew where she was. When she was awake, I could calm her down. Something bad has happened to her."

"Do you think she's on drugs?"

"I thought so at first. Don't tell her but I searched her bag. It was hard because she hangs on to it even when she sleeps. I didn't find much."

"Any ID?"

"No, not even a social security card. There's a journal full of poems. I read some of them. They're lonely. I remember one about her sitting all day on the beach, watching the waves reach for something in the sand. She doesn't have any money, just a few bus tokens in her purse, some allergy pills, and other personal things."

"Well, we had better see if we can wake her. Would you mind trying that? We'll have students here in a little while, and we need to have her calmed by then. We also need to make some decisions. I'll go to the kitchen and get something ready for her to eat."

We went quietly down the hall to the lounge. She was still sleeping, curled in the same protective position. The light of day showed that much of her thinness was from malnutrition. I went back to the kitchen, mixed some orange juice, and began frying the eggs. Karen came in a little later.

"Is she awake?"

"Yes, but she doesn't want to see you yet. I told her we'd eat first. She's worried about paying. I told her it didn't matter, but she said she'd pay when she got a job. She wanted to know if you were tall. It's funny—when I said yes, she got a look in her eyes like a scared rabbit."

"That is strange, but I can't change my height. I'll try and talk to her sitting down. You better go back out there; it might make her nervous if she thinks we're in here plotting."

I finished the eggs, and Karen took breakfast in to our visitor. As I waited in the kitchen wondering why I was so nervous, I nibbled on an egg and drank some orange juice. They went down in a lump. Karen finally came back into the kitchen with the half-eaten remains of our guest's breakfast.

"You should be able to go on in now, but be cautious. She's really jumpy," Karen said.

I tried to be quiet on my way out, but the kitchen door closed faster than it should have. She stood up immediately and turned quickly in my direction. Her eyes were wide, fear straining them as they took in every detail of my face. She jerked her head from me to the front door and then back to me again. I stopped in the middle of the hall, feeling like I had as a little boy trying to walk up to a covey of quail. I tried to calm her:

"Don't be afraid," I said, "I don't want to hurt you."

She remained rigid, however, looking out the front door, then back at me. I could see the struggle in her eyes as her face moved from the door to me. Remembering what Karen said, I sat on the floor to see if that would ease the tension.

"I'll just sit here in the hall if you don't mind. I should be able to hear you, and you can tell me anything you want. We'd like to help you."

She stared at me as if she were trying to see inside me. Her eyes were steel-gray as they looked over me. Suddenly they stopped focusing on me, and for a moment her attention seemed to take her completely from the building. Karen chose that moment to back through the kitchen door. The girl's attention snapped back, went wild with fear, then calmed with recognition.

"This is the man I was telling you about, the reverend. He can help you, but you have to trust him."

I stood up slowly. She began to twist the cloth straps of her bag.

"Please," she said.

Her voice was high and unstable. It was the voice of a frightened ten-year-old coming from somewhere deep inside her.

"Please," she said.

I stopped, then sat down on the floor again about ten feet away from her.

"I'm going back into the kitchen," Karen said to her. "You can tell him what you want."

I watched her eyes follow Karen back into the kitchen as though she wanted to call her back. She turned to the front door again, then back to me.

"I need to leave," she finally said. It was more like a plea. "I don't like to be inside. I need to walk. I can't pay you for the food."

"You don't need to."

"I need to leave. I went to sleep. I'm sorry—I didn't mean to go to sleep here."

"That doesn't matter. Sit down. Let us help you. You can leave whenever you want."

I was pleading more than she was and wondered at the earnestness in my own voice. I didn't even know her name.

"I like to walk. I want to see the mountains," she whispered.

"I like to walk, too. Have you walked in the mountains before?"

A tiny flush of color came through her cheeks. She stopped twisting the cloth handles for a minute.

"I draw mountains. I did in Vermont . . ."

Then her eyes froze with terror again, and she rushed to the door. She stopped rigid, her fingers twisting the cloth handles of her bag, pulling them tighter and tighter.

"Please. I don't want to. Please!"

Her breath came so fast she seemed to draw oxygen out of the room. At the same time she kept pleading, "Please, please. I don't want to."

"Karen!" I called.

Karen came out of the kitchen and rushed down the hall to where she stood. Karen caught her, then wrapped her arms around her. I watched her go limp in Karen's arms as they sat down on the floor. She let the cloth bag slip from her lap and tears spilled down her cheeks without a sound. I could hear the traffic outside, the hum of the refrigerator, her breathing, but still no sob, no cry.

I stood up slowly, crossed over to them, and sat down on the floor. Karen's arms were still wrapped tightly around her, her head close to the girl's loose blonde wisps of hair.

# Chapter 2

*A*t moments like this I always feel awkward, and often retreat into silence. It seemed to work. After a while her tears ceased, and I looked at her hands twisted in the cloth handles of the bag. We sat that way until she stirred, and Karen loosened her arms.

"Are you the reverend? He told me I could get help from the reverend."

"I'm not really a reverend, just the institute director here."

I wasn't sure she had even heard me. She hadn't looked at me. She was turning her head to Karen, saying, "He told me I could get help from the reverend. He gave me a name and the address."

She reached for her bag but had difficulty trying to pull the bag closer to her. I nudged it a little to help. She grabbed it, jerking forward to shield it from me. The sudden movement obviously hurt her, and she pulled back, folding her arms over the baby, still clutching the bag. She closed her eyes and clenched her teeth with pain. Then she opened her lips a little and let her breath escape soundlessly back into the room.

"I won't look in it," I said cautiously. "Can I help you with it?"

She nodded, then watched nervously as I lifted the bag to an upright position next to her. It was heavy and probably weighed over twenty pounds.

"Are you hurt?" Karen asked. "Are you sick?"

"Sometimes the baby hurts me. Sometimes it won't let me sleep."

"We can get you a doctor," I volunteered.

"No."

She began twisting the handles again, staring down at the floor, her breathing coming faster. Karen slipped her arm around her once again, but she winced at the touch.

"I don't want a doctor until I have to . . . until the baby's ready to come. I don't want anyone to see me."

"You wanted your bag, remember?" I wanted to change the subject so she'd calm down again and the fear would leave her face. "You were going to show us an address. We don't need doctors now if you don't want to."

"I want to leave. I like to walk. I don't like to be inside."

"You said you talked to someone. Who sent you here?"

"He said the reverend would help. Are you the reverend?"

"I guess so."

She took a small purse from her bag and opened it. I wanted to get a look inside, but she waited until we both looked away, then opened it close to her body.

She pulled a gum wrapper from the dark of her purse and handed it to me. I opened it and saw the address of the institute. Underneath it was my last name. She pointed to it and said, "Is this you? He said this man would help."

Her face was calmer now, streaked with tears she had never wiped away.

"He liked to draw, too. I saw him drawing the mountains. I was afraid of him, but he was drawing and he smiled when he saw me watching him. When he stood up, he was big . . . then a man came . . ."

He eyes went wild again. Quickly I responded: "He liked to draw, too? You first saw him sitting down?"

It was too late. She was gone again, her eyes focused somewhere miles away.

"Please! No! Please!"

Karen held her once again as she began to rock back and forth. The two seemed to melt into each other. I waited until the rocking stopped.

"The boy at the mall liked to draw, too?" I said.

The question seemed to pass by her. After a moment she turned and gazed at me.

"The boy at the mall. You talked to a boy at the mall? He gave you the address?"

She slumped back against the door.

"He said the reverend helped him. He said you would believe me. Nobody else believes me."

I thought I knew who she was talking about. I wanted to ask, "Where did you talk to him? What does he look like?"

Six months earlier I had found a boy sleeping in his car in the institute parking lot one morning. It was an old, faded, green station wagon. I approached it cautiously. He was asleep in the back. All I could see was his face; his sleeping bag was cinched up around his head. It was an almost freezing Colorado October day. There were some cans of food and a few pots stacked in the corners of the station wagon on a pile of sketchpads. At his feet was a dented metal footlocker, a Coleman stove, and an ice chest. I guessed that he had been living in his car for weeks, maybe longer. I looked for beer cans before I knocked on the window. He opened his eyes slowly and stared at me without moving.

"You can't sleep here!" I told him.

He unzipped the bag and folded it down around his waist to reveal a wrinkled shirt tucked into a pair of swimming trunks. He rolled down the window and stuck out his hand. I took it timidly.

"I'm a member. I need a place to shower, and nobody's here during the night. I went to church last Sunday."

I didn't believe him. I suspected he was trying to con me. I didn't mind helping transients from Pearl Street, but I always demanded they be honest with me.

"You want to quiz me on Joseph Smith or the Book of Mormon?"

"No, I want you to be honest with me. You don't necessarily need to be a Mormon for me to help you."

"I'm not here for a handout. I'm a member. Can't I use the parking lot at night and the showers before I go to work?"

"Are you living in your car?" I asked it softer than I thought I would.

"For now. Just till I save enough to get an apartment."

He opened up the foot locker. It had some clothes in it but mostly books. He pulled out some church books and a worn Book of Mormon with the initials J. M. T. engraved on the front.

"See. I'm a member."

"What's your name?"

"Adam."

"Adam what?"

"Just Adam."

"Okay, Adam, I believe you. Why don't you come inside? Take your shower, and then we can get to know each other better."

I liked him. There was no explanation for it. Maybe it sprang from some inner need to help people, some quirk of my character—or maybe I would have liked him no matter what condition I found him in.

I never questioned him about his name, so he remained Adam to me and always will. I tried to get him to move in with one of our students until he could find his own place, but he wouldn't do it until he had enough money to pay rent. He was saving money to pay off some kind of debt to his parents. He had once had quite a bank account, he told me, but the debt was apparently beyond his ability to pay. He worked as a janitor in the evenings and weekends. I tried to find out about his parents and family, but he avoided talking about them.

"I can't go home," he would say, then change the subject.

I would shoot baskets with him in the morning before he moved his car to make room for the students and allowed him to use the showers and lockers. He continued to sleep in his car even when the October chill turned to November snows. He ate out of cans in his car or sometimes in our lounge. I offered him the use of the kitchen when I was in the building, but he preferred his Coleman stove and ice chest.

"I'm not really a student," he said. "I don't want to get you in any trouble."

He started once to tell me what he was running from but got flustered and took off. He came back an hour later.

"You're not good for me," he said. "I want to talk to you, and I can't. I can't tell you. Don't wait for me to talk with that patient

15

I'm-trying-to-understand-you look on your face. I can't tell you anything about me. You've got to understand that I can't."

"I don't need to know anything, Adam."

"If I told you, things would change, so I'm going to go before I tell you."

He left the institute and came back a few hours later with his trunk full of books.

"You can have these for the institute. I don't have room in the car for them. Also, I drew this for you."

He dropped a chalk pastel drawing on my desk of the Flatirons that rise above Boulder. It was a winter scene with the rocks and trees just dusted with snow. I had told him once I loved to see them that way. He turned to go.

"Are you leaving?"

"I quit today. I'm going to sell my car."

"Why don't you go home?"

"Not yet. I haven't got things straightened up yet. I'll be in to see you tomorrow."

But it was the last I heard from him. Those experiences, his books, still on my shelf, came back to me as I sat with the elfin girl on the floor. Maybe she had seen him, knew him from Pearl Street. I wanted to find out if she knew anything more about him. I wondered why she had even let him talk to her.

"The boy who gave you the address . . ."

"He told me to come here."

"Yes, but the boy who gave you the address. Did he have light hair? Did he have a scar on his hand and arm?"

"He said I could trust you."

"You talked to him on the Mall. Was that yesterday?"

"The Mall is open. You can walk there. I need to leave

now. Please let me leave. Then I'll come back. I can't stay here anymore."

She stood up and walked toward the door, her heavy cloth bag pulling her shoulder down. I stood up and followed her. She turned and faced me.

"Please don't stop me. I just need to leave. I'll come back, I promise. He said I could trust you."

"You wanted help."

"I just need help for the baby, but it isn't time yet. I need to walk. I can't stay here. Please let me walk."

"Can I walk with you? Or Karen? You can tell us what you need for the baby. I have four little children—I know a little bit about babies."

She smiled for the first time, a faint smile, like a memory. Her teeth appeared straight and white.

"Four?"

"Yes. Eight, seven, four, and two."

She turned and walked out the front door.

"Call LDS Social Services, Karen. The number's in the directory on my desk. Tell them what's going on and ask them what to do. Ask if somebody will come up. I'm a teacher, not a psychologist."

Then I hurried out the door, remembered how afraid she was and walked cautiously, following her slowly about a half-step behind.

"There are some pretty places to walk on this campus," I ventured. "They have a fountain and a pool with turtles, surrounded with trees and flowers."

"I'd like the pond. I like the ocean."

She didn't say a thing again until we had crossed the campus and reached the pond. I wondered how many rules I was breaking by walking alone with her, especially since she was young and fairly attractive—and pregnant. It was an open invitation for rumors, but I felt compelled to help her. I tried to be careful because I was afraid she would lapse into one of her nightmare spells again. Yet, outside in the sun she seemed almost normal. I also wondered what she could tell me about Adam.

When we arrived at the pond, she stopped and stared in the water for a while, watching a turtle slip from a floating log into the water.

"What are your children's names?" she asked.

"I have two girls. Tiffany is the oldest, then Elizabeth; we call her Bethany. I have two sons, Joseph and Joshua. My wife's name is Ruth. Most people call me Ben. What shall I call you?"

She shook her head and stared back into the water.

"It's hard to talk to somebody whose name you don't know."

"Why do you want to know my name?"

She moved away from me a few steps.

"I'll just call you Laurel. Is that okay?" It was my wife's middle name and the only one I could think of on the spur of the moment.

"Yes," she replied after thinking about the name for a few seconds.

She stayed a few feet away from me. I could feel that she was very tense, so I began to tell her about my children and the funny things they sometimes did or said. She laughed like a little child, then stopped suddenly and stared into the water. I would struggle to pull her happy memories back to the surface, memories that would bring her laughter and let her look at me and not into the dark water of the pond.

"Do you know what my daughter Tiffany told me the other day, Laurel? She gave me a definition of fat. She tried to put on

Bethany's clothes by mistake, and when she zipped up the front, it caught on her stomach. She said, 'Being fat is when your stomach gets caught in your zipper.'"

I laughed, remembering the effect of Tiffany's words on the whole family at the time, but then I caught Laurel's distressed and worried look. It stopped my merriment.

"Was she hurt?" she asked. "It must have hurt."

"Only a little," I said. "She didn't even cry."

But the story had broken the mood, and we both lapsed back into melancholy. We watched a family of turtles climb onto the mud bank. She made me shoo them back into the water because she was afraid the boys on campus would throw rocks at them and kill them. I tried to tell her they wouldn't, that this was a place the students came to think and be alone, but she didn't relax until they were back in the water. She was glad the trees were tall so the scores of squirrels that lived on campus could climb to safety.

"They're safe here, Laurel. See that window ledge in the ivy. I know the secretary in that building. She buys sunflower seeds, ten pounds every week, just to keep the squirrels happy. She's made them all welfare cases, but nobody hurts them. They'll come right up to you if you want them to."

"I want to see the lady."

"All right. She'd love to talk to you, and you can watch the squirrels feed."

We left the pond and circled to the front of the building, climbed the steps and stood in the doorway. She stopped and looked down the corridor.

"I don't want to go inside. I don't want to see the lady."

"Maybe we can see her through the window."

We walked around to the side of the building. I waved at my

friend, and she waved back. It eased the tension again. We walked back to the stone bridge that crossed the pond and stopped in the middle. I felt I was beginning to gain her trust so I took a chance and asked her about Adam.

"Did you like the boy at the mall who told you to come and see me?"

"He didn't talk loud."

"No, he wouldn't. Did he say where he was staying? I would really like to talk to him."

"I don't know. He sent me here."

"Was he—"

"—I don't know."

I backed off. Maybe later there would be time to find out more about Adam, if it was him.

"Laurel, what kind of help did you tell him you needed? There are some things I can't help you with, but I can find the people who will. We have people trained to help, and we have some good Mormon doctors in the area."

"No doctors till I have the baby. I don't want anybody else. The boy said I could trust you. He said *you* would help. You help me. I don't want anyone else."

"I will—all I can—but I need you to trust me enough to tell me what I need to know."

She turned and looked over the wall of the stone bridge into the waters of the pond and gripped the handles of her bag once again.

"I don't know. Sometimes people say all the right things and then they hurt you. They're always going to hurt you even when you . . ."

The tears came again without a sound as her face filled with pain.

"Look!" I pointed into the pond. "There's the turtle family again. See the little ones swimming behind the mother?"

She smiled when she saw them struggling to keep up, and she leaned further over the stone wall of the bridge to see them better.

"Watch them dive," I whispered as I dropped a tiny pebble into the water. I remembered as I dropped it she was concerned about the boys on campus throwing rocks at the turtles, but she didn't seem to notice and laughed when the shells turned and slid under the water as the growing ripples moved over the surface of the pond.

"Reverend," she finally said. "I can't trust anyone."

"You trusted the boy on the mall, didn't you?"

"He could draw. I showed him one of my pictures. He gave me an address."

I was clutching at straws. "My wife draws. She's probably not much taller than you. We live in a big house with lots of windows. Across the street there's a pond with ducks and other birds. Sometimes we even see a pair of blue herons. There aren't many houses close to the pond. You can see green rolling hills right up to the Rockies. Would you like to see my family, just for an hour or so?"

She looked into the water again, watching the ripples from the pebble finally reaching the shore. I thought she was picturing what I was describing because a little smile came and then disappeared.

"If I want to leave?"

"We'll take you wherever you want."

"I ride the bus."

"Laurel, you're going to have a baby soon. You need a place to rest and some good food so you can be strong for the baby."

"I'm going to give the baby away."

"We don't need to talk about that now. Let's talk about that later."

"Can I call you reverend?"

"If you want. What shall I really call you?"

She left the side of the stone wall and walked across the bridge before she stopped and watched me. Then she stared down at her own reflection.

"Laurel. I like Laurel."

"Laurel. Do you trust me enough to let me carry your bag? It looks so heavy for you."

She smoothed the handles between her thumb and finger, nodded, then dropped both hands at her side, letting the bag slip to the ground. I walked up to her, hesitated a moment, and picked up the bag.

# Chapter 3

The institute stood near the corner of one of the busiest streets in Boulder. It was a two-story building sitting on a gradual rise. When we finally arrived at the front steps, Laurel could see the students in the hallways and lounge through the double glass doors and shrank down the steps, grabbing the handles of her bag as it hung from my hand. It was evident she didn't want to go back into the institute. We walked to the side of the building where the parking lot was located. I showed her my car and carefully placed her bag in the back seat where she could see it.

"Laurel, would you mind if Karen came with us? I'm sure she is concerned, and she is a good friend of my family. I need to go to Denver and teach a class this afternoon. Maybe you would feel more comfortable with my wife if Karen were there."

"I'm tired."

"You can rest in the back seat while we drive. You can sleep when we get to the house. Should I bring Karen?"

"Karen's nice."

"Yes, she is. If you'll wait a minute, I'll go get her and phone my wife so she'll know we're coming."

I helped her into the car, then ran into the institute and found Karen.

"Did you call LDS Social Services?" I asked.

"Yes."

"What did they say we should do? Did you tell them she wasn't a member?"

"Does it matter?"

"I don't know; it could. What did they say?"

"They said they might work with her, but they need to talk to you. Here's the number. Ask for a Brother Curtis."

"I can't phone now. She's waiting in the car. I'm taking her home, and I need you to go with me. Will you?"

"Okay, but Brother Curtis said it would be best if you could talk her into going to a member's home. He gave me the names of some families that volunteer to have anyone come without more than a few hours' notice. One is here in Boulder."

"I'm afraid she'll run off if we change our plans. Besides, she can barely stand on her feet from carrying that bag. I don't think she's seen a doctor yet. Will you go out and sit with her while I call my wife, please?"

She started to go, then turned and asked, "Are they all this way?"

"Who?"

"The people who come in here every spring?"

"I hope not, Karen. I don't think so."

I picked up the phone and dialed our number. It rang twice before I heard the familiar hello.

"Ruth, I'm bringing the girl home that stayed here last night."

"Do you have to?"

"When you see her, you'll understand. I've got a class in

Denver in an hour, and she'll run off if we don't find her some-place to rest."

"I'm in the middle of the wash, and the house is a mess. The boys have turned the living room into a city with their blocks and cars. Can't you keep her there till this afternoon?"

"I don't think she'll wait that long. She's exhausted. Besides, I have confidence in your ability to turn chaos into calm in a mat-ter of minutes. I've seen you do it when a car drives up."

"What do you want me to do with her?"

"If I knew the answer to that, I'd tell you, but I don't. You'll know better what to do with her than I will. Please!"

"Okay, but drive slow."

I hung up and walked to the car. Karen was in the back seat with Laurel. By the time we were out of the parking lot and on the freeway, Laurel was asleep. Twenty-five minutes later I pulled into our driveway. Laurel was still asleep. I got out, closed the door quietly, and dashed into the house. Ruth was sitting calmly in a spotless house, surrounded by the boys—who were even bathed.

"I knew you could do it," I said.

"But my stomach's in knots," she replied.

"You'll know what to do. I have faith in you."

Laurel was awake, and Karen brought her up the walk. I could hear her telling Karen she needed to leave. When she got to the door, her eyes were wide with fear. I pointed to the pond across the street and to the ducks. It helped a little, but the panic never left her. My son ran out the door.

"I'm Joseph. You're going to stay with us and sleep in Tiffany's room. You want me to show it to you?"

With the magic only a four-year-old possesses, he took her bag and struggled up the stairs with it. She followed a few feet behind, smiling faintly, then stopping when she saw Ruth. They were the same size. They looked at each other a few moments. Laurel smiled again, while Ruth picked up our baby. Ruth was nervous, I could see it in her eyes, but she took Laurel with her free hand and helped her inside.

"You're the reverend's wife?"

The panic in her voice was gradually subsiding.

"Yes. My name is Ruth. This little guy is Joshua. Ben always forgets to introduce people. That and not being able to find the car in a parking lot are his only two failings."

"He showed me the pond with the turtles."

"We have a pond here, too. When you feel up to it, we can walk over and see it."

My son came down the stairs again and took her hand. She jumped a little, then saw who it was.

"Come on and see your room," he said.

"Joseph," my wife said, "don't pull on . . ."

"Laurel," I said.

"That's a lovely name. Joseph, be careful! Let go of her hand. She's going to have a baby soon. We'll take her upstairs later."

"My mom had a baby once." Then pointing to Joshua he said, "He's right there."

Laurel smiled, and Joseph, sensing he had said something smart, reveled in his moment of glory. He took the bottom of his shirt and stretched it over his head, which caused a rebuke from his mother, but now brought a laugh from Laurel. I thought, *Keep it up, Joseph, you're the best ally we've got.*

I felt comfortable when I had to leave for my class. As I left, everyone was going into the kitchen for lunch. Ruth had already set the table.

As I drove into Denver, I felt I could relax for the first time in hours. The tension was beginning to drain away. I taught my class and went back to the institute in Boulder. Karen was back in the office. She told me she had taken the bus back when Laurel went to sleep. My son had pulled her up the stairs to see the room, and Ruth had handled everything else well.

Laurel's mention of Adam had given me a faint hope that I might see him on Pearl Street, so I told Karen I was going home, took my car, and drove down there.

I remembered the first time I walked down Pearl Street with Adam. He was going to treat me to lunch. We came across a six- or seven-year-old boy, lost and on the verge of tearful panic. I thought it strange a parent would lose a young child on Pearl Street. Adam sat down on the sidewalk next to him and began to ask him questions. He took a piece of paper out of his pocket and began to draw. I watched him draw clowns, animals, and trains with ease for ten minutes. Whatever the boy wanted Adam would draw. When the boy would look nervous, Adam would say, "We'll just sit here and draw pictures till your parents find you. They'll be looking for you." Finally a worried set of parents came running up, thanked us quickly, and took the boy by the hand. As they moved away we could hear the father scolding the boy for wandering off.

Adam turned to me and asked, "Did you ever get lost in a mall?"

"My cousins took me fishing one day along a riverbank. I was lost for an hour. I've never forgotten it." I was always conscious of my need to find out as much as I could about Adam and looked for opportunities to probe his personality.

"Did you ever get lost, Adam?" I asked.

"Once." He was still looking at the boy.

"And?"

"Kids don't get lost because they want to. They just like to look at the things in the stores because they've never seen them before. Parents expect their children to always be looking at them. Maybe the parents should look at the kids instead."

I understood as the memory came back why Laurel would have accepted Adam. Adam understood children. When I had to take Joseph to work with me one afternoon, Adam took care of him for me. He sat him on his shoulders and let him shoot baskets with a tennis ball in the gym.

I walked up and down the mall four or five times peering into every little shop until I finally realized I was making a fool of myself. I headed for home. Halfway down the freeway I remembered I hadn't called LDS Social Services. I took the next off-ramp, turned around, and drove back to Boulder. By the time I got there and phoned, they had closed. I railed against myself for my stupidity, thought for a bit, then decided that Ruth could handle any crisis. I'd call again in the morning.

When I walked in the front door, Laurel was standing in the middle of the room staring at the door, and my wife was standing next to her trying to calm her down. Laurel's eyes were wide and hysterical again. My children were standing around them, quiet and tense, trying to figure out why everyone was so excited.

"See," my wife said, "it's just Ben. The garage door always makes a noise when it drops. Nobody's going to hurt us. It's just my husband."

"Daddy, what's the matter?" Tiffany asked.

"You didn't lock the doors. He didn't knock," Laurel said.

"What's the matter?" Bethany asked.

"Why don't you lock the door? People can get in."

"I have a key, Laurel," I said. "The door was locked. I opened it with my key. See?"

I held my keys up. "Nobody can get in. We have two locks on the outside doors. I'll lock them now so you can see."

As I went to lock the doors, my wife asked as gently as she could, "What are you afraid of, Laurel?"

"Please. I need to leave. I can't stay. Please let me leave."

My wife, using that soft but emphatic tone I had heard her use with the children, said, "Laurel, there's no place to go. No one will hurt you. You need to stay."

I thought that would backfire, but it seemed to work. Laurel looked at Ruth, then took a deep breath.

"I'm sorry, Ruth. You're nice. I like your children."

"What happened?" Joseph asked.

"Go watch cartoons, kids," I said.

"They're over."

"Isn't there something you can find to do in the basement till dinner?"

"We want to stay here."

I threatened them with a look which suggested terrible punishments, and they walked quickly away.

"Do you want to lie down again, Laurel?" my wife asked her. "Yes."

"Let me help you up the stairs."

"No, I'm all right."

She started up the stairs, then turned and looked at my wife. Her eyes were wet again. She stood there for what seemed a long time just looking at Ruth, then she lowered her head.

"I'm sorry. I'm just trouble. You're nice people. I'll leave if you want me to."

The tears were coming again. Ruth walked up the stairs and turned her without effort.

"You're no trouble, at least none that we can't handle."

Ten minutes later, my wife came back down the stairs into the living room. I had just finished explaining to the children in the basement that they had to be very quiet and help us with Laurel.

"She's asleep again," Ruth said and dropped down in a chair.

"I guess I've handed you a big one this time. I'm sorry, Ruth. I have to admit it was a relief to walk out of here this afternoon knowing you were worrying about her."

"Every noise scares her. When the kids came home, banging the doors and yelling, I thought she was going to scream."

"I've talked to them."

"They've really been more of a help. The girls took her down to the pond."

"Alone?"

"I went down a few minutes later. She was laughing and pointing at the ducks. They think she's wonderful. Bethany wanted to know if we could keep her. She volunteered her bed and says she'll sleep on the floor."

"If only it were that easy."

"Ben, what are we going to do with her? What's happened to her? It's something she won't accept. When she remembers . . ."

"I know. We'll have to wait for LDS Social Services. I tried to call them at the office, but they were closed. I could try the bishop. Maybe he knows how to contact them after hours."

"She needs to see a doctor. Because of the baby, I'm worried about those allergy pills she takes. She took one this afternoon. I didn't want to worry her more so I tried to ask her about them without arousing suspicion. She's been taking them all along. I'm afraid of the effect they may have on the baby."

"I didn't even think of that."

"She needs to be examined. She plans on waiting until the

baby comes and then have the police take her to a hospital. I don't think she has any idea what having a baby is like. When I mention a doctor, she becomes terrified."

"I should've warned you."

"So what are we going to do with her? I tried to feed her lunch. She couldn't keep it down. Maybe there's something wrong with her physically."

"Did you find out anything else about her? Where she came from? Her family? Anything?"

"She slept most of the afternoon except when the girls took her down to the pond. I didn't know what to ask her. Little things set her off."

"I'll go call the bishop and see if we can get the number for Brother Curtis at LDS Social Services."

It took me four phone calls to get in touch with Brother Curtis. After an hour's conversation I convinced him to come up the next afternoon. Somehow we needed to persuade Laurel to see him.

Laurel slept through supper and was still sleeping by eleven P.M. when we went to bed. At about two in the morning she began screaming. We rushed into her room. She was holding her stomach, pulling her legs up, then slowly letting them back down. She stopped screaming when she saw us and tried to hold her breath. The pain forced it out again, and she cried out once more. Her face was covered with perspiration. I hurried to shut the doors to the children's rooms and walked back in as Ruth knelt down by the bed.

"Laurel," Ruth asked, "what's the matter? Did you have a nightmare? Are you sick?"

"I need to get up. It's hurting. The baby is hurting me."

"Are you having labor pains?"

"I don't know."

"Is the baby pushing?"

She didn't answer. She closed her eyes and bit her lip. I watched her legs slide back and forth under the blankets.

"Ben, I think she's in labor."

"Do you want me to call an ambulance?"

Laurel's eyes flew open, and she tried to sit up in bed.

"No! No ambulance! I don't want them to touch me. I can't have the baby. Not now."

Ruth tried to calm her.

"Laurel. If you're in labor, you're going to have the baby whether you want to or not. We can't help you with that. You'll need a doctor."

"Please don't let me have it now. I'm not ready. I don't want a doctor. Please, you help me."

"Then calm down and tell me what the pains feel like."

"I can't."

"Has your water broken yet?"

"What does that mean?"

A new fear began to grow in her eyes. My wife's voice was trying to ease it.

"The baby rests in a protection of water. When it's ready to come, the water breaks, and you'll feel it."

"I don't want a doctor, I don't want them . . ."

"Laurel." Ruth's voice was emphatic again. "Has it?"

"I don't know. Oh, please, please."

"I'm going to put my hand on your stomach to see if you're having contractions."

Laurel screamed again, this time in terror, not pain, and hit Ruth on the side of the head. She hit her once more and tried to climb out of bed. I grabbed her hands and held them tightly while Ruth tried to hold her shoulders. It was a mistake. She went wild.

"Don't hit me. Please, no, please!"

I released her hands immediately. She looked at me with a stare of total hate. It made me back up into the doorway of the room.

"We won't hurt you, Laurel," Ruth said. "But we can't help you unless you let us. I just want to see if you're having contractions and how hard they are."

"I don't want her to touch me." She was still staring at me, but the look changed to pleading.

"I won't touch you, Laurel. I won't. Lie back. Tell me what the pains feel like."

"I can't."

"Laurel," it was Ruth's commanding voice, the one filled with resolve and self-confidence, "if you don't talk to us, I'll have to have my husband call an ambulance, and they will take you to a hospital now."

I stood quietly in the doorway and gladly let her handle it.

"Please, don't! I'm sorry I hit you. Can you make the pain stop? I don't want an ambulance."

"Do the pains come in waves every few minutes? Do they cramp and move inside?"

"Yes."

"How long have they been coming?"

"Since I came up here before dinner."

"You haven't been sleeping?"

"Sometimes, then the pains would wake me up. When you came in, I pretended to be asleep so you wouldn't know."

"Laurel, I think you're going to have your baby tonight."

"No, this happened once in the room in Denver, but it stopped."

Ruth looked at me still standing in the doorway.

"Ben, get me a watch—one with a second hand so we can time the pains. You'd better call the Jensens so Kathy can come over and watch the kids if we need to go to the hospital."

"I don't want to go to the hospital. I want you to help me," Laurel said.

"We won't take you until we have to, but if you're going to have the baby, you have to be in the hospital. We won't worry about it now. Okay, Laurel?"

"You won't leave? Will you be with me? And the reverend?"

"I'll go right into the delivery room with you, and my husband can be right outside the door."

Another contraction came. I didn't stay to watch it but ran to our bedroom to get my watch. I could hear Ruth talking Laurel through the pains with a soft, steady voice. I checked the time, then ran downstairs and called the Jensens so they would be ready. When I got back upstairs, Ruth had turned off the bedroom light. The hall light flooded the room dimly. We timed the next six contractions. They were coming about every seven minutes. She was dropping off to sleep between each one.

"Do you want to go to the hospital?" I whispered to Ruth.

"If they get down to three minutes, we will."

The next pain came eight minutes later, the one after that, ten. When the last one finished, Ruth talked to Laurel.

"I think it's false labor. We won't have to go tonight unless they start again. You'll tell me if they start again, won't you?"

"Yes."

"Are you feeling better?"

"Tired."

Her eyes were closed, and she was breathing deeply.

"I'll stay here with you until the pains are completely gone. You rest now."

"Ruth," her eyes were still closed as she spoke, "who will take my baby when it's born?"

"The doctors will if you'll let them. They're very gentle, and the nurse will wash and feed the baby, and then you'll get to hold it. Tomorrow, if you want, we could drive down to the hospital and let you see how everything works so you won't be frightened. You can see the tiny babies if you want."

"I don't mean that. I mean who will keep my baby?"

"You will. Nobody will take it away from you."

"I can't keep it."

"You're the mother."

"I didn't want to be a mother. I wouldn't be a good mother. Not like you. I want the baby to have a good mother and father like you and the reverend."

"Don't worry about it tonight. We can talk in the morning."

The tears were slipping through her closed lids, but she kept them shut. I stepped a little further into the room. She licked her lips and started talking again.

"Will you find my baby a home? With a father who would love it and not be mean to it?"

"Now is not the time to talk about it. Sleep now."

"I don't have a job. They won't let you keep a baby if you don't have a job. I had one in Florida, but they made me quit when they saw the baby was growing. It made me mad. I can work. They won't give me a job in Denver. I wanted to go to Estes Park and get a job because I didn't have any money. I like the mountains. There were mountains in Vermont. I . . ."

The tears came with little sobs this time. Ruth kissed her on the forehead, smoothed down the strands of hair, and she fell asleep.

# Chapter 4

Ruth spent the rest of the night next to Laurel's bed on the floor. I called the Jensens and told them it was a false alarm, then climbed back into bed and lay awake listening for any sound coming from the other bedroom. At seven, Laurel woke up. Ruth tried to get her to take a shower, but she refused. I made breakfast for the kids and put the girls on the bus for school. Ruth came down to the kitchen about 8:30 while Laurel was dressing. I was trying to figure out a way to talk to Laurel about Brother Curtis. Ruth and I were talking about it when she came down the stairs carrying her bag, twisting it around her fingers. She stopped halfway on the stairs and looked toward the front door.

"I need to leave," she said with apologetic finality, as though it were a decree she couldn't help but obey. Her control seemed to be slipping. She had tried to put her hair up in a bun on the top of her head, but had missed whole sections. Her eyes were darting about, her hands shaking, but she tried to mask her weakness by holding the heavy bag still.

"Why, Laurel?" I asked.

"You can't make me stay. I can go when I want. You said you'd let me."

"Will you have breakfast first?"

"I'm not hungry."

"You haven't eaten much."

"I need to leave. Please!"

She walked down the last few steps and stopped again. Her face was weary and helpless. I tried again just to hear a voice.

"Laurel, where are you going?"

"To the mountains. They'll give me a job there."

"How will you get there?"

"I'll find a bus."

"Do you have enough money? We can give you some if you'll let us."

She looked trapped, like a rabbit in a snare. I felt like I was pushing the jaws tighter, but I didn't want to lose her. She had ceased to be a responsibility. Somehow Laurel had become ours. I was desperate and looked at Ruth. Her face was as weary, torn and helpless as my own.

"Don't you understand? I just need to leave. Please let me go."

The scared, trapped look was gone. In its place now was a child pleading.

"I have to teach a class this morning. Let us take you up to Boulder. That's on the way to Estes Park. Can we do that much? Ruth can drop me off at the institute, then if you want, she'll drive you up into the mountains."

"You'll let me leave?"

"If that's what you feel you need to do. Can we give you our number in case you need help later? All you have is the institute address."

Ruth wrote the number out on a slip of paper, tucked it into

Laurel's bag, then said, "Let me get some clothes on, a bottle for Joshua and get Joseph's coat, then we'll go."

"Can I go outside and sit by the pond?"

"Of course."

I watched her walk out the door and down the hill to the pond. The ducks were swimming on it. She stood like a sentry guarding the quiet waters until Ruth was dressed. We walked down to her side and told her we were ready if she still wanted to go. Without speaking, still holding the heavy bundle of her clothes bag, she walked back up the hill and crawled into the back seat. Joseph sat next to her. Perhaps he sensed a mood of depression, for he too was silent. After we drove onto the freeway she spoke.

"I just need to walk, that's all. I want to go back to the mall where the boy was."

She looked out the window at the passing green of the hills, but the motion of the car quickly rocked her to sleep. She was still sleeping when we pulled into the institute parking lot. Her head was tipped back over the seat, her mouth open, her breath labored. Ruth said she'd remain with her in the car and stay at the institute until she woke up. I took the boys in with me and tried to keep them from the typewriters and other machines while I threw a lesson together for my morning class. Every few minutes one of my students would peek in and ask me about our newest Pearl Street visitor. Karen had spread the word, and there was comforting apprehension and concern. Some went outside to say "hi" to my wife and see Laurel. A half hour later I went outside again. She was still asleep, and Ruth was reading in the front seat.

I had forgotten that I had an appointment with a police officer that morning. We had had trouble with illegal parking in the lot. The officer arrived a few minutes before my class began. We went outside to look at the parking lot and to discuss the problem. It took only a few minutes, but it made me late for my class. I hurried back into the building and asked Karen to babysit while I tore upstairs.

When class was over, I wanted to check on Ruth, but the students asked about Laurel. I spent fifteen minutes telling them what I knew and suggesting how they should act if she came into the building with my wife. When they were satisfied, I hurried downstairs and out to the car. It was empty. Thinking they had gone for a walk, I looked to see if her bag was there, but it too was gone. I couldn't see Ruth or Laurel anywhere, so I went back to talk with Karen.

"Karen, did you see my wife go? Did she leave a message?"

Karen was coloring pictures with my sons.

"No. I thought she was still in the car with Laurel."

"They're both gone. I can't figure it out."

"Maybe they went for a walk."

"I hope so."

I waited an hour, then began to get worried. Ruth finally came into the building two hours later. She was flushed and hot from running, out of breath, and alone. I could see that she'd been crying.

"I'm sorry, Ben, I lost her."

"How?" I almost shouted, then immediately felt bad.

"She woke up when the police car came. She got that look when she saw you talking to the officer. She insisted on knowing what you were doing. I told her I thought it had something to do with the institute parking problem. When you went back inside, she wanted to walk. I tried to walk with her. She kept saying she wanted a bus. I think the officer scared her. I told her she shouldn't worry, but she wouldn't stop; she kept walking, lugging that bag around with her. She wouldn't even let me carry it."

"So where is she?"

"Ben, she's an adult. I couldn't make her stay with me or come back to the institute. We walked to a bus stop below the university, and she seemed to calm down, but when the bus came, she climbed on. She had a few tokens in her purse. I didn't have any money because I left everything in the car when she got out. I couldn't make her stay. I didn't mean to lose her. I'm sorry . . . I didn't even see which bus she got on."

I tried to comfort her as best I could, but it wasn't enough. Karen entered the office during our conversation to find out what had happened to Laurel. We talked for a bit, then I said, "There's one thing we haven't faced. It's hard to believe, but maybe she's running from something. Why else would she be afraid of the police?"

"She hasn't done anything wrong!" Karen said emphatically.

"What if she goes into labor again, Ben?"

"We could get the students to help you look for her," Karen suggested. "We could split them up and look through the malls and campus."

"All right. She likes open places, especially Pearl Street, and she liked the turtle pond."

Within a few minutes we had five groups going in different directions. Karen said Laurel only had a few bus tokens and no money, so we got a bus schedule and figured out how far she could go. Ruth took Karen and the baby in the car and drove all those routes. I took Joseph and walked up and down the mall, looking for Adam as well. I kept worrying that maybe Laurel had done something wrong, then I felt guilty about that thought.

Eventually, to settle my questions, I walked back to the institute and dialed the police.

"Yes?" a bored voice said. I pictured an overworked clerk facing a pile of vandalism and petty theft reports. I introduced myself, then started.

"Yesterday a girl came into our building. She was nervous, sometimes on the verge of hysteria. At times, she seemed to be having some sort of flashbacks."

"Did you check for drugs?"

"We didn't find any, and I don't think she would use them. She seemed proper, clean. I don't know how to describe it. I just don't think she would use drugs."

"Not all drug addicts are dirty and poorly dressed, Mr. Christianson."

"She was about eight months pregnant, maybe more. I don't think she'd use drugs."

"What do you want, Mr. Christianson?"

"She's run away."

"You just met her yesterday? Is she a runaway?"

"Well, she's over eighteen."

"Do you wish to report a missing person?"

"No. There was an officer out today . . ."

"What did he tell you to do?"

"He came about a parking problem, but when she saw him, she was terrified. That's when she ran off. I wondered. . . I'm afraid that maybe she's done something wrong somewhere. I just thought I'd find out. She's mentioned Florida and Vermont, and I think she also had a room somewhere in Denver."

The guilt rose like a hot wave in my throat. I checked to see if the office doors were closed, wondering if Karen had come back and was listening on the other side.

"Did she confess to a crime?" the voice droned.

"No. I just thought maybe you could check. I don't think she's done anything, but . . . well, I just wanted to check."

"Would you like to come down to the station and make a statement?"

"I'd rather not. We have some people looking for her, and I need to help."

"What is the relationship of this girl to you?"

There was just a hint of accusation in the voice that made me feel uneasy.

"No relation. She's just . . . she came into the building. We had her out to the house for the night. . . . No relation, just a girl from the mall."

"A transient? I wouldn't worry too much, then."

"Please. It's important."

"If you'll just give me a description of her, I'll check it out for you."

I described Laurel as best I could. I had trouble again when I couldn't give him a name. Finally he said he had enough information and hung up. A half-hour later, one of the groups came back. They hadn't found anything. Fifteen minutes after that, Ruth and Karen returned. They hadn't seen her. They had even checked the hospitals just in case. We sat around the institute waiting for a miracle that would bring her back through the door. I didn't mention I'd called the police and kept worrying that the phone would ring, the bored voice would ask to speak to me, and I'd have to explain what I'd done.

Then Brother Curtis came in. In all the confusion I had forgotten to call and tell him.

"We lost her," I explained. The words sounded strange. She

was an adult. We hadn't really lost her, she'd simply gone away, and yet "We lost her" seemed to be the only appropriate remark.

We talked with Brother Curtis for about an hour. He spent most of the time telling Ruth she shouldn't feel guilty. I knew my wife better than he did, and knew it wouldn't do any good. She would feel bad anyway, and it would last for days.

"She might come back," he said, "or call if she gets really desperate, especially if she's that close to having a baby and hasn't eaten. This is a normal reaction in this type of case. She knows she can find help with you; that will stay with her. You did right in giving her your number."

We talked a little about the baby being adopted if she did return. He assured us arrangements could be made; the procedure wasn't complicated.

Ruth and I took the boys home, and Karen said she'd stay late at the institute in case Laurel came back. Dinner that night was a solemn affair. Nobody said much. We had a special prayer and put the kids in bed. Every time the phone rang, we jumped. About 8:30 it rang once then stopped. Ruth and I looked at each other without talking, then both stared at the phone.

"If it's her, Ruth, it would be better if you answered it."

A moment later it rang again. Ruth eased it off the hook and said, "Hello?"

"Who is it?" I asked, trying to keep calm.

"Hello. This is the Christianson's. This is Ruth."

I tore upstairs and picked up the bedroom phone as quietly as I could. Ruth was still the only one talking.

"Is this Laurel?" she asked. There was no answer, but I could hear dim voices in the background. I stifled the urge to talk, knowing Ruth would handle it better, and two voices might frighten her if it was Laurel. I was convinced it was. My mind raced to place the background noises.

"Laurel? This is Ruth. Where are you? Let us come and get you."

Still silence hummed through the line with the background noises getting fainter.

"Laurel?" Ruth's voice pleaded into the receiver. "We've been so worried. Are you all right?"

"No."

"Laurel." My wife's voice had never sounded so gentle. "Laurel," she repeated, "let us come and get you. Please."

"I ran away from you."

"No, you just got scared. We all get scared sometimes."

"The reverend's mad."

"No, Laurel. He's not mad, believe me. He's been worried. Even the children want you to come back. Where are you? Let us come and get you."

"He'll be mad. He'll yell at me."

"No. He never yells. He's right here. Do you want to talk to him? He's not mad at all, just worried."

"I just want to talk to you."

"Are you all right, Laurel? We looked all over Boulder for you."

"I needed to leave. I rode the bus all day. The first driver was nice; he let me stay, but the new one made me get off."

"Where, Laurel? Where are you?"

I dropped my hand over the mouthpiece and nearly shouted, "She's at the bus station!" I wanted to jump up and race to Boulder while Ruth tried to keep her on the phone, but decided against it. I put the receiver back to my ear.

"Will you let us come and pick you up and bring you home?"

"My home was in Ohio. He would yell at me. He was mean. Will the reverend yell at me?"

"No, Laurel, he never yells."

"He grabbed my arms. He scared me."

"He didn't mean to."

"You won't let him yell at me or grab my arms?"

"Laurel, what's the matter? Please let us come and get you."

"I'm sick. The baby's hurting me. I'm hungry. Will you bring me some of the rolls you gave me yesterday?"

Her voice was weak. It faded so low I wondered how Ruth was picking it up, but she didn't seem to be missing anything.

"We'll leave right now. But you have to tell me where you are."

"Will you bring the reverend?"

"Not if you don't want him to come."

"He would feel bad."

"He wants what is best."

"Ruth, do you think I'm bad?"

"No, Laurel. I just want to help you. I want you to trust me so you won't feel you need to leave. It was my fault you left, not yours."

"I'm in Boulder."

"We'll come right now. Where should we meet you?"

"Where the buses come in. You can bring the reverend. He would feel bad."

"Stay right there. Don't stand up if you're feeling sick again. We'll be there in twenty minutes."

"I'm hungry."

"We'll bring you something to eat and drink. Laurel, you won't leave, will you?"

"I won't run away."

"We're leaving right now."

"Ruth, I'm not a bad person. You don't need the police. Tell the reverend he doesn't need the police."

"That was for the parking at the institute. He didn't call the police about you, Laurel. We know you're not a bad person. You're just a little frightened. We all get frightened. We'll come and get you now. You'll stay?"

"Where the buses come in."

She hung up. I tore downstairs. Ruth was sitting in a kitchen chair crying. I gave her a kiss and a hug, then raced next door to ask a startled neighbor if she would sit with the kids for an hour.

Within three minutes we were on our way to Boulder with some rolls and orange juice. When we got to the bus station, the parking lot was dark and empty except for one or two cars. We could see through the windows to the worn benches inside. In the middle of one sat Laurel. She was all alone, her cloth bag resting on her lap, her fingers twisted in the straps. There were some scattered newspapers on the bench next to her and around her feet. She was looking down at them with a vacant stare. The bun on the top of her head was half down, but she didn't brush her hair away or pull it back.

We went through the door slowly so it wouldn't bang. It didn't matter. Laurel didn't even look up when Ruth stopped in front of her. Ruth sat down next to her and hugged her.

"Laurel," she whispered. "Are you awfully sick? Are you having the pains again?"

Ruth hugged her tighter. Laurel let her without resistance. She was still staring into the newspapers.

"I'll go with you," she barely said.

I took the heavy bag from her hands. She didn't resist.

"The pains are gone. I'm just tired. I want to go to sleep. They wouldn't let me sleep on the bus. I'm hungry."

"We have some rolls in the car and some orange juice."

"They wouldn't let me stay on the bus."

A man from the ticket counter came over to us.

"Does she belong to you?" he asked.

"Yes," I said.

"Sister?"

"No, a friend."

"She's been sitting there for two hours. We had to order her off the bus. She got really mad, but she only paid one fare. I know she's pregnant, but we couldn't let her ride the route over and over again. She wouldn't tell us where she wanted to go; she kept saying, 'I don't want to get off yet.' What's the matter with her anyway?"

"She's confused," I explained. "We'll take her with us. If you want me to, I'll pay the extra fares."

"Never mind. You take her; that will be enough."

During the entire conversation, Laurel sat next to Ruth, limp and motionless as if she hadn't heard a syllable. I bent down and slowly took her hand.

"Let me help you out to the car, Laurel," I said. "I've got your bag."

I let her weight rest between us, and we walked her to the car. Ruth climbed into the back seat with her. She gave Laurel the plate with the rolls and took the tinfoil off. Before I had pulled out of the bus station she had finished one and was starting on another. Ruth tried to get her to slow down, but she was starving. A few streets later she had finished four and drank all the orange juice. It was too much. She began cramping.

"I'm going to be sick again, Ruth. Please don't let me be sick again."

"I'll take us over to the institute," I said.

I ran a stop sign and risked several tickets but got us to the institute within minutes. I ran in ahead and asked all the students studying in the lounge if they would mind going upstairs for a few minutes. We were bringing Laurel in, and I didn't want fear added to her problems. When we helped Laurel into the building, the lounge was empty. Ruth took her to the restroom. I sat down at the foot of the steps. I could hear Laurel crying and asking Ruth to make her stop and Ruth's soothing voice calming her. Then there was only crying, and the institute students crept down the stairs.

"Is she going to be all right?" one of them asked.

"I don't know. We need to get her to a doctor, but she's terrified."

"My mother's a midwife and a registered nurse. Would she see her?"

It was worth a try. Maybe if she just came without Laurel knowing, Laurel would allow her to examine her. I called the nurse, explained the problem briefly and asked if she could meet us at our house. After giving a few directions I hung up. Laurel and Ruth were still in the restroom. I could hear Ruth's voice soft and steady but couldn't understand what she was saying. The students sat in silent groups. When the door finally opened, Ruth was white-faced but calm. She almost carried Laurel through the doorway. Laurel's eyes were closed, her face ashen.

"Laurel," I begged, "let us take you to the doctor."

"No! I want to go home with you. I won't be sick anymore. The baby isn't coming. Ruth will take care of me. Please."

I looked at my wife. She shook her head. I took Laurel's other arm and helped her across the lounge.

"We'll just take you home. You'll be all right there," Ruth whispered. "You ate too fast, that's all. You'll be all right after you sleep."

We stopped midway across the lounge and let her lean against the back of the couch. Then we continued on to the car. She was asleep before I circled the car and climbed into the driver's seat.

We drove down the freeway in the dark, hearing only her breathing and the sound of the air speeding past the car. Halfway home I asked Ruth how Laurel was doing.

"She's really out."

"Can she hear us talking?"

"I doubt it. Laurel? Laurel, can you hear me?"

"She needs medical attention, Ruth."

"She won't see a doctor."

"One of the student's mothers is a midwife and nurse. I called her while you were in the bathroom. She's coming over tonight."

"Who is it?"

"Sister Hancock."

"I wish you had talked with me first."

"How could I?"

"She won't like it."

"If we ask her, she will always say no. Maybe this way she'll let her at least talk with her."

"All right, but we'll tell her she's a friend who is also a nurse; that we were really worried about her being sick tonight and that Sister Hancock only wants to talk to her to make sure the baby is okay. We'll tell Sister Hancock not to touch her."

When I rolled into the driveway, Laurel woke up. She was having trouble holding her head up. I went into the house to relieve our neighbor in case Laurel panicked. I heard Ruth yelling for me so I rushed back to the car. Laurel was hanging halfway out of the door, almost lying on the driveway, and my wife was struggling to keep her head off the pavement.

"She passed out, Ben, while she was getting out of the car. I can't hold her. The baby is against the door. I slapped her to bring her to. Forgive me, but I slapped her. I even shook her, but she wouldn't come out of it. I didn't slap her hard, but she was falling out of the car. What else could I do?"

Ruth was in tears.

"It's all right," I said, "I'll carry her inside. Sister Hancock will be here any minute. If she says take her to a hospital, whether Laurel wants to or not, we'll take her to the emergency room."

I picked her up as carefully as I knew how. I expected her to weigh more, but it was like carrying my daughter. Ruth supported her head as we carried her into the house and laid her on the couch. Tiffany came downstairs.

"You've found Laurel!"

"Yes, dear. You go back to bed," I said.

"Is she sleeping?"

"Yes, for now. You go on back to bed. You can talk to her in the morning."

"Is she going to the hospital?"

"I don't know. You don't need to worry about that. Hurry up to bed."

Tiffany went slowly back up the stairs, stopping every few steps to look back. By the time her bedroom door closed, Laurel had come to, and Sister Hancock walked through the front door. Our neighbor was still standing on the front porch looking in, wanting to help. Laurel saw everyone, and terror came into her eyes.

"Who are they?" she almost screamed.

Our neighbor backed off the porch and excused herself.

"You were so sick," Ruth said, "Ben called our friend. Her name is Sister Hancock. She's a nurse, not a doctor. She's helped lots of ladies with babies. Maybe she can help you."

"Please, don't let her." Laurel was begging now.

"We are so worried about you, Laurel, and about your baby. You fainted in the driveway and fell out of the car. I couldn't hold you. Please let Sister Hancock talk to you."

"No, I don't want her."

"I won't hurt you, Laurel," Sister Hancock said and approached cautiously.

"There's nothing to be afraid of."

"I'm afraid. Oh, Ruth, I'm afraid."

"Everybody is afraid with their first baby," said Sister Hancock. "It's normal to be afraid, but it's a beautiful thing to bring a life into the world."

"I don't want a baby. I'm not ready, Ruth. I don't want her to look at me. I don't want her to touch me."

"I'll just talk to you then, Laurel. Would that be okay if we just talked?"

"I won't talk to her."

"You just tell me how you've been feeling. Brother Christianson told me you had some labor pains last night. Can we talk about those?"

"I want to leave. I don't want to stay here. Don't let the reverend make me stay and talk to her. Please, Ruth, send her away."

Ruth turned, looked at me and began to cry.

"I can't stand it, Ben."

I turned to Sister Hancock with a look of total hopelessness. Ruth was kneeling next to Laurel, holding her.

"Brother Christianson," Sister Hancock said, "she's dependent on your wife. She'll never let anyone see her or open up to anyone who can help her medically if Ruth's in the room. Maybe if you both left she would have to trust me, and I can help her. She has to be examined. She appears to be full term. We don't have any idea what the baby's condition is, or hers either for that matter. She shouldn't go into a delivery room unexamined."

Laurel heard the conversation then grabbed on to my wife. Her eyes were now filled with terror. She was pleading with Ruth.

"We better make it another time," I said weakly.

"It will always be this way. Believe me it's for the best. Take your wife, Brother Christianson, so I can have a chance of her transferring her trust. This is beyond your or your wife's ability to handle."

"Ruth, maybe she's right."

Laurel wouldn't let go. Her fingers grabbed the material of Ruth's coat and twisted it into tight bundles.

"Sister Christianson, I know this is hard for you, but you need to do what's best for her."

Ruth made a vain, half-hearted effort to get free.

"Laurel, listen to me," she said.

"No."

"Laurel, she's a nurse. She won't hurt you. You can trust her. We'll be right outside."

"Please. You said you wouldn't hurt me on the phone. You said you would help me."

"You'll need to go to a neighbor's house and give me at least an hour with her," continued Sister Hancock. "As long as you're in the house . . ."

"I don't . . ."

"Laurel," it was Ruth's emphatic voice again, but it lacked

strength this time. "You've just got to let someone check you. Just to make sure everything is all right. Just so we won't worry."

"Is this your first baby? Have you been sick? Have you had false labor?" Sister Hancock asked.

"I'm not sick. I don't hurt. Please, Ruth, make her go away. Make the reverend go away."

"We can't do it, Ben, she's terrified."

"Ruth, maybe we're not helping? Maybe we're just making things worse?"

"She's terrified, can't you both see that?"

"Sometimes you can't go by your feelings, Sister Christianson." Ruth gave in.

"All right! Laurel, you're going to have to let Sister Hancock at least talk to you. That's all you have to do, just talk to her, like you did with me last night."

Ruth pulled away. I put my arm around her. Laurel was whining, hurt and terrified, her fingers twisting as if the familiar cloth handles were between them.

"I can't talk to her. She won't understand. I'll tell you why I'm afraid. I'll tell you if you'll stay. Please! Let me tell you."

"Will you at least talk to Sister Hancock? She's a nurse, Laurel."

"Send her away. I don't want her to hear. Just you and the reverend can stay. I don't want the nurse. Please."

I turned to Sister Hancock.

"Maybe it will be better if we talk to her first. There's a couch in the family room if you want to sit down. I'm sorry, but maybe this will be best."

"I'll stay in case you need any help."

She walked into the family room and left us alone with Laurel. Ruth was kneeling by her side again. Laurel had taken her hand. She grasped it tightly. When I kneeled down with her, she took mine also. Her fingers and palms were cold, covered with moisture. Her eyes were closed.

"Laurel," Ruth whispered, "she's gone. What do you want to tell us?"

Laurel kept her eyes closed. Her sentences came out one by one, each with increased tension while her fingers grew tighter around our hands.

"I ran away from home. I ran away from my father. He would always yell at me. He said I was stupid. He said I was . . . I ran away, and he couldn't do anything because I was old enough."

There was hate in her voice. The same strong emotion I had felt last night.

"I ran away to Vermont. It was near the mountains. I loved the mountains. I worked and rented an apartment. I took care of myself. I drew and played a piano in one of the little shops. They let me. I was alone, but I wasn't afraid because I had friends, and we would go to the mountains. But one night . . ."

She tightened her fingers on my hand.

"I went to get a pizza . . ."

Her eyes jerked open. She stared straight into the ceiling.

"There was a pizza place around the corner. I just wanted a pizza because I was hungry, but it was late. I knew the man who ran it. He was a friend, but it was late . . ."

Perspiration began to crawl down her forehead, holding the hair in wet strings.

"When I left, the street was dark, but there were street lights . . . but one of the buildings . . . the light was burned out. No! The light was burned out. They were walking behind me, two men. They said words to me, but I kept walking. I was afraid—I'm afraid, Ruth. Please help me. What can I do? They're whispering at me, Ruth. I'm afraid because the streetlight is burned out. They're going to hurt me, Ruth, I know it. Please stop them. They're hurting me! Oh, please, stop, stop! I want to leave. I have to walk. I only wanted to get a pizza, but the light was out. Ruth, make them stop! Please! PLEASE!"

Laurel arched across the couch, shaking her head back and forth, her face white, her eyes now pressed shut. Then her fingers and body released their tension, and she cried hard and deep and long with a sorrow that seemed beyond grief, perhaps beyond hope. My throat closed around the words I couldn't have said, would never be able to say, because they would never be enough.

Strange things come to our minds when we're under great stress. I sat with my hands in her fingers and remembered a college philosophy class. We sat around one day and discussed with sophomoric maturity the question of why there was pain and suffering in the world, why God did nothing about it.

I didn't even understand the question then, but I was so sure I knew the answers. Now there were no answers. There was just pain. I remembered my professor and his graduate assistant, and knew that they didn't know the answers either, because those who had known that kind of pain wouldn't talk about it, wouldn't be able to talk about it if they wanted to, and those who had lived it wouldn't know how to begin to form the questions. We made a philosopher's toy that afternoon, to be bandied around book-lined university offices and chalk-filled classrooms by people who didn't understand God any more than they understood pain. Pain and suffering were just ideas to them, so of course, God was just an idea, too.

I thought of the men by the burned-out streetlight and felt a powerful surge of hate, an angry, vengeful, blinding hatred for men whose names and faces I would never see or know. The hatred overcame the grief until I heard her speak again and hearing her words created the grief all over again.

"I walked home and sat on the floor in the middle of the room with all the lights out. I got some scissors from a drawer and cut my clothes up into little pieces and left them on the floor. I stayed there until it was morning. Then I cut the telephone cord into little pieces because I didn't want to tell anybody. I took all I could carry in my bag and rode a bus to Florida, till I couldn't go any more. I couldn't tell anybody because I was so far away. They never got caught, and when they do it again, it will be my fault. I did wrong, Ruth, I'm sorry. I got the scissors and I . . ."

She began to shake once again with her tears. Ruth held her closer, kissed her temples, trying vainly to smooth her hair back over her ears. I finally found a voice.

"Nobody would blame you, Laurel, for not being able to tell. Nobody . . ."

"But I did wrong, and then in Florida I was afraid because I started getting sick. I was afraid of what it meant. I couldn't go to work, but I had to. I knew they would find out. They would make me leave my job when they found out. I didn't want to have a baby, Ruth. Nobody would believe me. They would think I was bad and take my job away. They would think I did evil things. I hated the baby. I shouldn't hate it, but I hate it. I'm bad. Why did it have to come? It won't let me forget. I try to forget, and it won't let me. I can't forget because it hurts me. Why did God send me a baby like this, Reverend? Why did He send it? I can't keep it because I will always remember. I would yell at the baby and be mean to it like my dad. You must find another home where they won't yell and be mean, where it won't be afraid, so even when it was in trouble and wanted to go home, it could go home and not be afraid."

Ruth rocked her in her arms until she dropped my hand. Laurel was asleep. I waited until Ruth let her go, stood up, and walked quietly to the closet to get a blanket. Then we went to the basement, found an old cot, and set it up next to the couch. I brought Ruth's pillow and a blanket down from our bedroom.

I went to the family room and thanked Sister Hancock, telling her we'd better try another time and walked her to her car. When I returned, I realized Ruth hadn't said a word. She lay down on the cot and stared up at the ceiling, tears wetting the hair at her temples. I sat in the chair and watched her, searching in my mind for words to say, but I still had none. Ruth wouldn't have wanted to hear them if I had. When she finally closed her eyes I turned the lights out and went to check on the children. They were sleeping soundly, but I wondered as I lingered in each room how another Father felt as He looked at His sleeping children. Then, while watching my sons side by side asleep in their beds, almost without realizing, I asked the question. I waited. I could hear my sons' breathing in the darkness of their room. There were no other sounds in the house. I listened for a hint of movement downstairs, but everything was still. I wondered as I waited if life was such a precious gift that we had to buy it with suffering and pain at the price of one another. I wanted to cry, but I couldn't.

# Chapter 5

The next few days saw the beginnings of a change in Laurel. The reasons were complex, of course, and probably due to a number of things. Most of all, I suppose, was the relief of being able to relive with someone else an experience she was struggling to accept. The terror in her eyes seemed to subside except when she was surprised by sudden loud noises. We asked the children to sing or whistle as they came home from school and to knock instead of ringing the bell or barging in. Laurel still insisted we lock the doors, especially at night and when I was at work. Ruth told me that several times during the day Laurel would check to see that the doors were locked. The last thing she did before climbing the stairs at night was to check the front, back, and garage door.

Ruth checked on Laurel each night before she went to bed as she did our children. One night she found her standing by the bedroom window looking into the backyard. She asked nervously, "Do you think anyone would be able to climb up here at night?"

Ruth assured her it was too high, but Laurel replied, "They could bring a ladder."

Despite these moments, Laurel appeared to be much more at ease. There were no more labor pains, and we had hopes she would let a doctor examine her.

It was different with Ruth. She didn't want to talk about that night. I knew she was deeply troubled about it. She would go about the everyday housework with a too-businesslike manner. It bothered me.

A day or two later, some institute students brought a box of gifts into my office for Laurel. They were concerned that they had scared her off the day the police came and wanted her to know they were her friends. I took them home that night and gave them to Laurel. She was overwhelmed, and a bit suspicious. She kept saying, "But they don't even know me." I told her that Karen had told them about her and that they were good students. They had even asked if she could come to church Sunday morning to see them. She cried then.

The box contained wrapped presents of art supplies and baby clothes. When she opened them and saw the baby clothes, she cried again, almost unconsciously twisting the material slightly in her fingers. She looked at Ruth and said, "We could give these to the family, couldn't we?"

My wife took the clothes from her hands and smoothed the tiny wrinkles.

"I have to talk to the man from your church about the baby, don't I? I can't just talk to you?"

We had mentioned Brother Curtis to her the day before, but just lightly.

"When you feel ready," Ruth answered.

"Don't you know anybody who would want a baby?"

"I'm not sure we could have any say in the matter, Laurel," I said.

"I want it to be a good family." She looked at the yellow sleeper in my wife's hands. "One where the father doesn't yell."

Her words about a good family wanting a baby touched a memory. As a boy I had spent many weekends in the summer with my cousin Chad and his family on the beach. No amount of time will erase from my mind the memories of swimming in the surf, feeling the power of the waves rippling down my back when I dove under them; picking live, twisting creatures from the tide pools; rolling in the warm sand after hours of shivering in the May surf; or grunion hunting in the moonlight.

I played and swam most often with Chad. He was a little older than I and looked out for me. One summer evening Chad, his brothers, and a friend dared me to swim out past the breakers with them. I was twelve and a good swimmer, but afraid. Their teasing was too much. I gave in and went with them. It was too far for me. I couldn't get back to shore, and the terror I felt drained me of what little strength I had. Chad tried to help me, but the tide continued to pull us out. He kept telling me I'd be all right, to swim toward the pier. Finally I reached the pier, grabbed the first post, and hung tight. Following his instructions, I let go with each new wave and allowed them to sweep me to the next post. They were covered with mussels which cut me, but I made it back to shore, where we both collapsed in the sand. We lay there until it grew dark and the stars came into view. With that experience, Chad became almost a brother to me. All this flooded back as Laurel said, "Don't you know anybody who would want a baby?"

Chad and his wife had been married for over five years without having a child. They both wanted one desperately. For the last two years, they had worked with the California foster home program, trying to adopt one or another of the children they had cared for, but each time difficulties came up. Recently, they had had to give up a two-year-old boy they had raised since he was three months old.

I called Brother Curtis the next morning. He was concerned about Laurel and delighted to know she was getting better. I told him what we had learned the night before, and about Laurel's desire that Ruth and I place the baby in a good home. I asked him about Chad and Jenni in California. He stopped me halfway through my enthusiastic description.

"Enough," he said. "You've convinced me to look at them and see what can be done. There's a chance we can do it, but I need to do some checking, and I'd like to talk with Laurel—if you can convince her to see me."

"Should I tell her about my cousin?"

"No. Let me do some checking. It isn't good for the mother to know where the baby is going. You could share with her your memories of the family, however. They will be good for her."

We spent three hours that night sharing slides and old photographs with Laurel and the children. I told all the stories I remembered, especially about Chad. Laurel immersed herself in them completely, laughing and asking questions. Sometimes she'd get a faraway look as if we'd struck a little coil of memory in her past.

We closed the evening with the kids singing her a song. Then Laurel asked if she could play a song she had written. We nodded, surprised, and she went to the piano, sat down, then stared intensely at the keys. Finally Ruth went up to her and lightly touched her shoulder.

"Laurel?"

"I'll play it now, but I don't want to sing the words. I can't right now."

She touched her fingers to the keys and began to play. As I watched her fingers barely touch the keys, it seemed as if she was not playing the notes, but coaxing them from the hidden strings. It was a wistful tune, melancholy, in a minor key. Her head slowly swayed from side to side as she played; her eyes closed, the music coming from her instead of the piano. By the end of the song she was humming the melody. When she finished she didn't take her hands from the keys, but lifted them lightly from key to key as if still playing. Finally she turned to us, her eyes staring into another world.

"I'm sleepy. I'm going to bed now. You don't have to wait for me."

Then she climbed the stairs without looking at us and softly closed her door.

When the kids were finally down and asleep, Ruth and I talked. I told her my idea about Chad and Jenni. She approved. She suggested it would be a way of keeping in touch with the baby, like a grandchild. The suggestion seemed to lift her spirits.

"That was a different song," I said.

"It was a difficult piece. I couldn't play it, especially without music. She's talented."

Ruth played the piano beautifully. She had given lessons for years. Her saying that Laurel was able to play something she couldn't seemed high praise.

"I wonder where she learned," I said.

"She must have had lessons of some kind, but she's also got a natural talent. She's hovered around that piano all day. She'd sit down and stare at the keys and then get up. I asked her if she played. 'Once.' That's all she said, and I couldn't get anything else out of her. Then she'd walk down to the pond for awhile and come back and sit down and put her fingers on the keys and move them from key to key. I think she composes things in her mind and can hear what she's thinking without playing. 'If you want to play,' I said, 'please do. It won't disturb Joshua.' 'No, I don't feel like it,' she'd say. Then she'd get up again and walk back down to the pond. She'd stay there for an hour, then come back and sit down again and move her fingers over the keys without making a sound. She'd sway her head from side to side and close her eyes like she did tonight, humming the same melody. It surprised me when she said she would play for us tonight. She can draw, too. I saw some of her rough sketches while I was cleaning out her bag to wash her clothes."

The next morning at the institute I received three calls. The first was from the Boulder police. As far as they could tell, Laurel was not running from a crime. I felt a little ashamed as I listened since I now knew the real reason for her fears. They had also checked the missing persons file and had no record of anyone looking for her. I said "Thank you" and almost hung up, but I wondered if her parents had filed a missing persons report.

"I've since learned that her home is in Ohio. Do you think you could run another check knowing that?"

"Mr. Christianson, the search we made was thorough. If a report had been filed, we'd know it."

"Thank you."

"Perhaps you should notify the parents if you know where they are. I'm sure they would be concerned."

Since I didn't know who her parents were, I said thank you and hung up. I thought about Laurel's parents and wondered what they were like. Did they ever think about their daughter?

Did they ever wonder where she was or what she was doing? Was she happy, or in trouble, or for all they knew, dead?

Laurel hated and feared her father. Her facial expressions on those few times she mentioned him convinced anyone watching of that, but her mother? She'd never mentioned her mother. Maybe she was dead, or absent, or maybe she too was afraid. I was lost in a reverie of questions until the phone rang again. I heard Brother Curtis's voice.

"Brother Christianson, I have some hopeful news for you. Things look very positive for your cousin. If they want the baby, I think we can arrange it. They haven't been contacted yet, but I've talked to California Social Services. Everything is complete from their past requests."

"That's fantastic!"

"We need Laurel's approval of course, and she'll need to sign some papers. I'll need to see her and explain the legal formalities."

"We'd like you to see her. I know she needs counseling, and we never know if we're doing the right thing."

"Would you see if you can convince her to let me talk to her? I'm sure I could help. I've dealt with similar cases."

"We'll try. I'll call you first thing tomorrow and let you know if I've succeeded."

"That will be fine. Keep building her trust. She's better off with a family she feels she can trust than anywhere else. How is her health?"

"It seems to be better. I believe we have a few more days before the baby will be born. We still need to get her to a doctor."

"I can suggest some to you that are very good."

"Brother Curtis, do you know if my cousin will be contacted? I'd like to talk to him a little."

"Brother Christianson, I'd be cautious if I were you. I need to talk to Laurel, and we have some initial legal agreements to make."

"I can't tell you how much I appreciate everything you've done so far. Thank you so very much."

"Thank you, Brother Christianson. We like to see things end happily for everybody, too. It's not always rewarding dealing only with problems."

"If the last few days are any indication of what your job is like, I'm glad I direct an institute."

"That's why it's nice to see this one begin to work out. Let's keep working and hoping."

I taught my noon class and then began work on some reports when the phone rang again. Karen couldn't get the caller's name, which she always did. She leaned in the door and said, "I don't know who it is. He won't give me his name but insists you'll want to talk to him."

I picked up the phone. "Hello."

"Brother Christianson. This is Adam. Do you remember me?"

"Of course I remember you. I've been thinking about you the last few days. I've even gone to the mall to look for you."

"That's where I am now. I'm calling from one of the shops."

"Why don't you come up to the institute?"

"I can't. I feel like a fool for just taking off last fall. I'd be embarrassed around the students."

"They wouldn't care. Every now and then one asks about you, and we've lent your books dozens of times."

"I'm glad you could use them."

"Come on over."

"I'd rather not."

"Okay. How are you?"

"I'm still trying to get my head on straight. I've been back East. I spent some time in Boston, but Boulder got to me so I drifted back this way."

"Have you been home?"

"I'm not ready for that yet. Maybe a little while longer."

"Have you contacted your parents?"

"I sent them a card from Boston awhile ago saying I was okay."

"Listen. Why don't I come on down to the mall. I'll treat you to lunch. There's a health food restaurant there that smells of cinnamon and orange . . ."

"Thanks anyway. I know the one you mean, but I've got some friends waiting. We're looking into some things . . . I just called . . . well, I just called."

"Do you want your books?" I was trying to keep him on the phone.

"No. You keep them. I don't have much use for them."

"Adam, I'd like to see you. Would you do this much for me? Just let me see you and talk to you. We don't need to talk about anything serious."

"I've still got to work some things out."

"Let me help you work them out."

"I need to do it on my own. It's better this way. I just wondered how everything was going."

"Everything is great. Listen, Adam, thank you for sending . . ."

"Brother Christianson, I'm sorry; my friends are here. Maybe I can call you in a few days when we get our plans made. Take it easy."

He hung up.

# Chapter 6

*I* sat for a few moments with the phone in my hand then put it down. I was tempted to get up and search the mall, but called Karen into the office instead. As she was coming through the door, I realized how badly I wanted to tell Adam about Laurel, but he hadn't given me the chance.

"Karen, if you were a parent and your child were an adult, but had left home, wouldn't you want to at least know where he was?"

"I'd want to, sure."

"That call was from a boy—a member of the Church—I knew a few months back. He's done something which makes him feel he can't go home. I don't think his parents know where he is or how he's doing. I don't even know his real name. He calls himself Adam. Do you think I ought to be making some kind of effort to find his parents? I never thought until now that maybe Adam's mom and dad are searching for him, too. Maybe I should see if there's a missing persons report on him."

"If I were his mother, I'd hope you'd do all you could."

"From a few things he's said, he's from somewhere out West.

I don't think it's California. He told me his family went there on vacations and what a big thing it was for him to see the beach. And I don't think he's from Utah because he said there weren't many members in his high school. Do you think if we typed a letter describing Adam, what we know about him, and sent it to all the stake presidents anywhere west of Colorado, anything would happen? We could eliminate Utah and California."

"It's a long shot. How many stakes would we have to write to?"

"We'll copy the letter. If nothing comes up, at least we'll feel we've tried."

I drafted the letter. It took a few hours of our time, but I felt a lot better. Then after they were mailed, I felt a little foolish that I was bothering such busy men, because all but one letter would be meaningless.

I left the institute about five. The weather had been threatening to deliver a typical Colorado afternoon spring snowstorm. The temperature was dropping rapidly, and flurries were falling by the time I pulled into our garage. I was late for dinner. Ruth was setting the table and mentioned Tiffany had gone over to her friend's house around the block. She had called there a few minutes earlier for her to come home.

I wanted to tell Ruth about Adam's call, but knew I wouldn't have time to tell her all I was thinking. Ruth had met Adam only once, but I had told her all about our conversations. She had often suggested things to me which helped me with Adam. I needed to know what she would think. I helped her set the table, then walked into the living room. Laurel was sitting at the piano playing very faintly. I recognized the music as the same song she had played the night before.

"She's played it all afternoon," my wife whispered to me.

I helped finish setting the table. Tiffany still wasn't home. It was snowing steadily now, and we both began to worry.

"I'll call again and see if she's left."

She dialed the number. I could still hear the faint sounds of the piano and Laurel's soft humming. I went into the living room and sat in the chair next to the piano. Laurel didn't seem to know I was there.

"My wife tells me that's a difficult piece," I interrupted. "She's taught lessons for years. Have you written any others?"

"Yes," she said without stopping. I expected more, but nothing else came.

"Like this one?" I said, trying to get her to talk a little.

"This one has words," she replied.

Ruth came into the room then. Her face was worried but controlled.

"Tiffany left over fifteen minutes ago. It's only a five-minute walk."

Laurel stopped playing and swung around on the seat. Her face was as worried as Ruth's. I found myself talking to her as much as to Ruth.

"I'll go out and find her. You know how she is; she likes to dawdle along the way. Five minutes or a half-hour is the same to her."

"It's snowing," Ruth said.

"It's getting dark," Laurel added, then stepped to the front window and looked across at the pond which was fading in the flurries. Then she looked up the street.

"I think I can see her," she said, "over there in the middle of the street by the lamp."

We looked to where she was pointing. There was Tiffany,

standing in the middle of the street, her hat off—which didn't surprise us—looking in the opposite direction.

"What's she doing in the middle of the road, Ben?"

"Beats me. I better go get her."

Just then the headlights of a car pulled into view. Tiffany didn't move. She began to wave her arms back and forth over her head.

"Get out of the road!" I yelled more to myself than anyone in the room. The car slowed then stopped in front of her. Laurel's face went white. She put her hand over her mouth and said, "Hurry! Go get her!"

The car backed up a few feet, then turned around. Tiffany didn't move. I ran down the street, putting my coat on as I ran. Back in the house, Ruth, Laurel, and by this time the other children were watching me out the window. The snow was falling harder now, big water-soaked flakes that melted as they landed on the street.

"Tiffany!" I yelled when I was about fifty feet away. "Get out of the street! How many times have we told you? That car had to turn around."

"I can't, Daddy!"

"What do you mean you can't?" I was getting angry.

"It would get run over." She pointed into the street a few feet in front of her. "The cars can't see it. They'd run it over."

I had reached her by this time. I looked where she was pointing. In the middle of the road was a wild duck from the pond. It was leaning a bit on one side, but it moved quick enough when I made a step toward it.

"It's hurt, Daddy. Can we take it home?"

Tiffany was like that. She even made me carry crickets out

of the house in a jar instead of killing them. During the summer their constant chirping nearly drove us crazy.

"It's wild, Tiffany. You can't keep wild ducks. It's not hurt too bad either, because when I walked up, it moved."

"Yes, it is, Daddy. It was here when we went to school this morning. It was hiding under that car, and it's still here now. Something must be really wrong or it would fly away. Maybe a car hit it."

"Are you sure it's the same duck? There are lots on the pond."

"It was brown like this one."

"Lots of ducks are brown. This one will be all right. Let's get home, we're getting wet."

"It's leaning like the one was this morning."

"Maybe ducks lean like that when they're in the middle of the street and it's snowing!"

"It's cold, and it's getting all wet."

"Ducks like to get wet, and they have feathers to keep them warm."

"Why wouldn't it move when the cars came?"

"Tiffany, how long have you been out here stopping cars?"

"Since I left Jensen's. One car backed out of a driveway and couldn't see the duck so I told them at their window."

"How many cars have you stopped?"

"Just three."

"Tiffany, we can't stand out in the middle of the street and wave cars around a duck."

"Can't we take it home and put it in the garage?"

"It will be all right, sweetheart."

"It's snowing, and it's hurt."

"Look, I'll make it fly so you'll know it's all right."

I walked toward the duck and waved my arms. I wondered

what Laurel and Ruth were thinking back at the window. They couldn't see the duck. It scampered to its feet—part of the webbing of one of them was torn—and half-flew, half-ran down the street before stopping again and settling down.

"See, Daddy. It's hurt. It can't fly."

"I guess you're right, but I don't know what we can do about it."

Another car turned onto our street. Before I could stop her, Tiffany ran ahead and flagged it down. I hurried after her and got there as she finished telling the driver there was a wounded duck in the street and not to hit it.

"Is it your duck, sweetheart?" the lady asked.

"We're going to take it home. It's from the pond."

"I'm sorry. You can go ahead if you want," I apologized.

"Oh, no. I'll go back the other way and take another street."

She backed up and turned around. I wondered again what the faces back in the window were thinking. I was getting wet. Big silver-dollar-sized crystals were sticking to my head. I jammed my hands into my pockets to keep them warm.

"We need to go in, Tiffany."

"And leave the duck?"

"What can we do?"

"We can take her in the garage so she won't get cold and wet. You can call an animal doctor."

Ruth was coming out of the house now. She was walking down the sidewalk with a *can't-you-handle-this?* air about her. I wanted to make a decision before she got there, so I took control and said, "All right, Tiffany, we'll try to chase it into the garage, but I'll need Bethany and Joseph. Let's go get them."

"What if another car comes?"

"Right. I'll run and get them, you watch the duck from the sidewalk."

I met Ruth halfway back.

"What are you two doing out here?"

"We're rescuing a duck," I answered, "from the wet and cold."

"You're what?"

"Your daughter has decided to champion the cause of a wounded duck. She's been out here waving cars away, and I can't talk her out of it. We're going to try to drive it into the garage, then we'll call someone. There's got to be some society that fixes downed mallards. What about Ducks Unlimited? Isn't that the sort of thing they should do?"

"Dinner's cold and Laurel is going wild again because you two are out in the dark in the street."

"Go on back and send Bethany and Joseph. I'll need them to turn the duck out of the street into the garage."

A few minutes later I had positioned my three oldest children along the street in a wide curve that led to the garage. Armed with two sticks of rolled-up newspaper, I got around the duck and started to slowly push it forward. It waddled awkwardly along the middle of the street in front of me. I had to bend over a little, and the cold flakes kept landing on the back of my neck. Occasionally one of the neighbors would look out the window to check the snowfall and wave. They never turned away. What would happen when I said, "I'm a Mormon. Would you like to know something about my church?" I could hear them saying, "Oh, you're the one who strung his children down the road in a snowstorm and herded a duck with newspapers into his garage."

After a cold twenty minutes of haphazard chasing we got the duck to the driveway. I looked up at the front window and saw Ruth holding the baby while laughing and pointing at me.

I knew she was telling him to look at his silly daddy. Laurel was laughing, too. Then the dog barked. He was at the back door that led into the garage. The duck stopped, turned around and looked nervously at me and the children.

"I knew we could get it here, Daddy," Tiffany assured me. "I've been praying and asking Heavenly Father to help us save the duck."

"Good," I said, then told Joseph to go inside and put the dog in the house. He was only four and never did get many instructions right. He thought I wanted him to let the dog out to chase the duck into the garage. Twelve seconds later the dog came bouncing out of the door, Joseph grinning behind him. Our dog stood all of six inches high and was two feet long. Still, he tore at the duck, which suddenly with amazing speed ran back into the street. The dog chased the duck with me screaming behind him. I caught the dog at the corner, brought him back, locked him in the basement and brought the kids in to warm up.

"But what about the duck, Daddy?" they were all asking. "It's in the street again."

I looked at Ruth, hoping for an ally.

"It's in the street again," she repeated and smiled. "Besides, dinner's already cold. You might as well try again, and," she whispered, "Joseph feels terrible."

I looked at Tiffany, then I looked at Ruth.

"Sometimes Heavenly Father needs a little help answering all the requests He gets, I guess. Let's go try again, kids."

I rolled the papers up again, and the four of us filed out the door and circled back down the street. At least the neighbors weren't watching this time. Once again, with snow dropping down my neck, I herded the duck down the street and onto the driveway. When we got the duck almost in the garage, Laurel came outside and stood watching on the front porch. Her being there plugged the last tiny hole of escape, and we watched with relief as webbed feet waddled into the garage and under the car. I closed the door and breathed a sigh of sheer delight. Laurel was smiling at me, and my children were cheering. We had to feed the duck immediately. She devoured a bowlful of the dog's wet, milk-soaked food before we could finally sit down to our own reheated dinner.

I noticed a change in Laurel. She was a little more light-hearted, less despairing. It was worth chasing a duck down the street twice.

When the kids were in bed, Laurel, Ruth, and I sat in the family room and talked. Laurel usually talked with Ruth about most things, but tonight she talked with me.

"Reverend?" (I had given up trying to change that.) "When the baby's born, could it live here with you and Ruth?"

She dropped her eyes immediately and entangled her fingers in the hem of her blouse. I looked at Ruth for help, then realized this was one I had to handle. I opened my mouth and hoped I'd say the right thing.

"Laurel. That's the most beautiful gift anyone has ever offered us. We love children—but there are better people than Ruth and I who for some reason can't have children. They have never felt the joy Ruth and I feel. They pray every day that God will send them a child or that they can adopt one."

"Why doesn't He send them one when they would be nice to it?"

"I don't know, Laurel, I . . ."

"Why am I having one when I don't want it?"

"I don't know the answer to that. I wish I did, but you can

have this baby for one of those couples, Laurel, and give them a wonderful gift."

"I want to give it to you and Ruth."

"We'd love to have your baby, but maybe someone else needs the joy and happiness your baby would bring them, somebody who can't have their own."

"But I wouldn't know them. I wouldn't know they were the right kind of people. I couldn't . . . I couldn't see the baby with a good family."

"No, you couldn't see it, but the adoption services would find a good home. I'll make sure of it. They feel it's best for both you and the baby and the new parents if the mother doesn't know where the baby goes."

"Would it be a family in your church?"

"Only if you want it to be. I talked to Brother Curtis today. He said he knows of a family that haven't been able to have children. They've tried for years, and they've tried to adopt. They want a baby very badly. They're members of our church, and they'd be good parents. They wouldn't yell or be mean. They live near a beach, close by their parents, so the baby would grow up right there with its grandparents. It could play in the sand and peek into the tide pools and when it got older, swim in the surf."

"Like you did in California?"

"Yes, kind of like that. There might even be some ducks nearby."

She smiled a little then, still twisting the hem of her blouse, keeping her eyes down. During the whole conversation she hadn't looked up.

"You wouldn't want the baby?"

"We'd love the baby, but they wouldn't let us have it when

we know you so well, when there are other couples who want children so desperately."

"It's my baby. Can't I say?"

"Laurel, maybe there's something else you should think about. Maybe you already have. Are you sure you want to give the baby up? Maybe you would like to keep the baby."

"Oh, no. It wouldn't have a father."

"Not now, but later, you might find someone and . . ."

"No! I won't get married. I can't get married."

"But there's no reason why later . . ."

"No!"

She looked at me this time, and my own eyes dropped. There was silence for some time, and then she continued.

"Anyway, it would be happier in a house near the ocean, with a daddy."

"It's your choice, Laurel. Whatever you want is what we want."

"I want it to have a daddy. It will need a daddy."

"The daddy that Brother Curtis mentioned sounded just right."

"Will he tell the baby when he gets big that he's not his real daddy?"

Her eyes brought her fear into the room again as her questions kept coming.

"Will he tell the baby it never had a real daddy? Will he tell it that God sent it where there wasn't love, not even from his mother, because . . ."

"Laurel, please, don't, please! He won't say those things. He won't know to tell them."

She was crying again, but not with terror; this time grief was taking over. I could feel my own rage swelling inside of me. Ruth stayed in her chair.

"Will it hate its mother because she didn't want it? Will he wonder all his life what she was like? Maybe they will tell it, it's their baby, and it will never know."

The tears kept coming. Ruth went to her and sat on the couch.

"Laurel," I struggled, "in our church we believe families can be together forever. Even when they die. So we build temples . . . maybe you've seen one . . . and children are sealed to their parents forever. To be sealed means to tie two people's lives so tightly together that nothing can untie the knot, like two drops of water coming together. This little baby you're going to have will be taken by its parents to one of our temples and sealed to them. That means no matter how it came into the world, no matter who its mother or father were, God makes it the new parent's child as if they had given birth to it themselves, and they love it as if it were their own child. Your baby will grow up believing these things, and it will comfort both the parents and the child. Do you understand?"

She looked at me, then at Ruth, and finally back in her lap as if she could see the baby already lying there.

"Reverend, I haven't eaten well. I've been sick a lot. I've had those pains. What if the baby is . . . what if it's not . . . not going to be all right?"

"We hope everything is fine. Though I'm sure the baby will be healthy, that's one reason we'd like you to see a doctor."

"But if it's not healthy because I've been sick, because I was afraid to see a doctor, if something's wrong with the baby, will they still want it?"

"I think from Brother Curtis's description of the couple they would still want it and would love it no matter what happened."

"I need to talk to Brother Curtis, don't I?"

"Yes."

She turned to Ruth.

"Ruth, I'll see the doctor now and Brother Curtis if you'll stay with me."

# Chapter 7

Saturday morning we phoned the doctor that Brother Curtis had suggested. We got an answering service. Even though Ruth explained the situation was serious, the earliest appointment they could arrange for us was Tuesday afternoon.

Ruth talked Laurel into letting her wash her hair. Ruth took the knotted bun out and combed her hair down. It appeared to be self-cut, nicked and irregular in a few places with longer strands reaching to her shoulders. It was thin and lusterless. Ruth combed and arranged it as best she could to hide the rough spots. Laurel wouldn't let her recut it. When Ruth finished, however, Laurel looked like a new person.

We decided to take Laurel and the children shopping. Since Laurel liked Pearl Street we took her there. I also had a faint hope that if we went there I might see Adam. There hadn't been much time to think about him since he'd called. I realized that I hadn't talked to Ruth as I had planned. Laurel's conversation had made me forget, but this morning he was on my mind like the gentle tapping on a door, a tapping so light it's not sure it wants to be heard.

We took the children because Laurel reacted better in public when the children were with us. Tiffany took Laurel's hand, and together they walked behind Ruth and I. We wanted to buy Laurel some new clothes since Ruth had been washing the two outfits Laurel had every day. She was nervous when her extra set of clothes was in the washing machine. Whenever Ruth finished, she would immediately arrange them in her cloth bag instead of the drawer we'd emptied for her.

"Look, there's a maternity store," Ruth said. "Why don't we buy you some new clothes?"

"I don't want you to."

"Laurel," I added, "it would be fun for us to do that for you and the money's not a problem."

"I don't want you to. I have my own."

"Only two outfits, Laurel," Ruth took over again. "Wouldn't you like some pretty new ones?"

"I have others." She stopped walking and nervously moved her eyes up and down the shops. We realized the significance of what she said, but Ruth spoke first.

"Laurel, do you have clothes somewhere else?"

"In my bag." She looked trapped, as if she had been caught breaking a law.

"Are you afraid? Please don't be."

We continued to walk down the shops. Laurel still walked with Tiffany, but her eyes stared down at their feet. A few moments later she stopped in the middle of the mall.

"I didn't mean to hide it from you." She stopped and looked down at Tiffany.

Ruth looked at me, then back at the kids and said, "Do you kids want something to drink? Two stores down there's a refreshment stand. Here's some money. We'll sit here and wait for you to come back."

We sat down, watching the kids while Laurel continued.

"I didn't feel safe. I had to have a place to go. I tried to go back there the day I ran away from you, only I didn't think and the bus was wrong. Then I didn't have any more money. I was going to walk from the station, but I got sick."

"Walk where?"

Laurel's eyes searched the shops again, then dropped back to the floor.

"Denver."

"You would have walked all the way to Denver? It's over thirty miles!"

Laurel looked at the shops again and rubbed her fingers along the side of the bench.

"Laurel," my wife asked, "we thought you came to Boulder from Florida."

"I came to Denver first because that's where the bus stopped. I tried to get a job, but they wouldn't give me one. I could work, but they wouldn't let me. I wanted to live in Estes Park, but you need a job because it costs a lot of money to live there."

"Do you have some things at the bus station?"

Her hands rubbed along the bench, and she continued to look at the shops.

"Do you want us to drive down and get them?" Ruth asked. At this moment the kids returned, laughing with their drinks. "Laurel, can we buy you a dress for church tomorrow? The kids are singing with the Primary in sacrament meeting. I'm sure they want you to hear them sing. Besides, you'll feel so much better in new clothes when you're going to have a baby."

The kids perked up and began to beg her to come. Tiffany

and Bethany took her hands at the mention of their singing, their smaller fingers closing quietly around hers. She smiled.

"Just one dress."

The children's approval drowned out Ruth's and my reply. We stood up and walked toward the maternity shop. When we got there, Ruth gave me a signal that meant, "Take the kids and get lost for a while." After ten years of marriage I had learned to read a lot in the way she waved her finger.

"Why don't you kids come with Daddy down to the bookstore and then the pet shop?"

It was a sure-fire strategy, one I knew would work as well as "Let's go get an ice cream cone." I figured I'd need to use that one later. The kids loved to look at the pop-up books, and there were dozens of them at the bookstore. They also loved poking their fingers at the puppies and hamsters and covering the fish tanks with fingerprints. Eventually I would be carefully asked, "Are all these yours?"

The children and I trailed off down the mall, leaving Ruth and Laurel alone. We stayed in the stores as long as the managers could stand us, then went to the toy department at Sears. An hour and a half later we got an ice cream cone, ate it as slowly as possible, then walked the long way back to the maternity shop. When we got there, Laurel stood in the front, smiling, trying to hold in her enthusiasm. She and Ruth had picked out a new dress and two blouses, all in light blues and yellows. Laurel had one on.

"How about some new shoes?" I suggested. Ruth glanced at me, winced a little, then smiled and nodded. Laurel looked a little nervous again.

"Shall we go?" I said. "There's a shoe store a few shops down having a sale. My wife never buys shoes that aren't on sale. You'll have to let us stay this time, though—we wore out the pet store and then went through all the pop-up books in the bookstore."

Ruth stepped up to Laurel and put her hand on her arm.

"You'll look a little silly wearing tennis shoes in a beautiful new dress; besides, you don't need to try them on. What's your shoe size?"

"They won't make me try them on?"

"They didn't here, did they? You just pick out what you want and tell them the size, or if you want, you can try them on yourself. The salesman doesn't need to help you."

I understood and went with the kids down the mall to the shoe store. I watched her try various shoes on, leaning against Ruth away from the salesman. The grief and anger returned. We bought her a pair of low heels for church and picked out a few things for the girls, then started for the car. Ruth mentioned, as we were walking back, that Laurel wouldn't go into the dressing rooms. She wouldn't even let the sales lady at the maternity shop hold the new clothes up to her.

"But she had the new blouse on?" I said.

"She slipped it on over her old one."

In the parking lot she walked close to Ruth and I.

"Thank you."

"Oh, it was more fun for me," Ruth answered.

"You weren't embarrassed that I wouldn't go in the little rooms? You weren't mad?"

"Goodness, no. I understand. If you're sure of the sizes, everything's fine."

"I know they're right."

"Well, you can try them on at home, all by yourself in the bedroom, then you can come downstairs and show us."

Laurel turned and got into the car. She smiled softly all the way home and held the girls' hands.

# Chapter 8

When we got home, Laurel folded her new clothes carefully and put them in the drawer. It was the first time she'd used the drawer, but the familiar cloth bag, always packed, lay by the side of the bed. Laurel lay down and took a long nap early in the afternoon while the kids went out to play. I called Brother Curtis. I told him Laurel had agreed to see him. I wanted him to come over that night, but he said Monday would be soon enough. Also, by then he would know more about Chad and Jenni.

I finally had a few moments with Ruth. "I got a phone call the other day from Adam. I wanted to tell you earlier, but there hasn't been much time."

"Is he in Boulder again, still sleeping in his car?"

"I don't know. He said before he left last time he was going to sell it. He's been to Boston, but he wouldn't say much."

"Has he gone home?"

"No, I don't think so."

We talked about Adam for a long while. I was surprised she remembered so much. I told her about the letters to the stake presidents. She approved but thought it was a long shot. Then she reminded me of something I had forgotten.

"Do you still have those little notes? Maybe if you went over them again, you could find a clue."

"Little notes?" I asked.

"With his questions on them—the ones he asked when you went into the mountains?"

I remembered the drives in the mountains and the questions. We would sit for long moments without saying a word. I tried to be patient and pretend the silences didn't bother me. I don't think Adam ever noticed. He was used to silence. Because he didn't feel comfortable talking in the office, we drove the canyons. He would talk, looking out the windows at the trees and rocks, never at me. Afterward would follow the long staring silences I dreaded. They would usually be followed by questions. Most of them didn't relate to what we had been talking about previously. I always feared answering them without knowing what lay behind them. He had a fascination with Old Testament stories and often the questions that followed the long silences dealt with them. It didn't take very many questions for me to realize that he knew the Old Testament better than I did. His questions were about Saul, David, Esau, Reuben—characters I would not have thought he noticed while reading. After hearing a few of these questions, I believed they held some kind of key so I kept them, written on small pieces of paper. I would go over them alone in my office and try to understand. One in particular had bothered me. He asked me who I thought had suffered most: David or Job. I answered Christ and when he didn't press me for another answer, wrote the question down and put it with the rest. I noticed, though, it was always the note that lingered in my hand the longest when I thought of Adam. When Adam didn't return after a few weeks, I threw them away and hadn't thought of them until Ruth brought them back to my attention.

"I guess I threw them away when I cleaned my desk."

"I don't know—they probably weren't important. I just wondered if this time maybe you would find something there to help him."

We ended the conversation, and Ruth busied herself with the children. I went into the living room with a notepad and tried to remember the questions I had saved, but most were gone from my memory.

About four that afternoon, Laurel woke up and came downstairs. She was wearing her new blouse. She had a tablet of white paper and some chalk pastels with her.

"I'd like to go down to the pond and draw. I'd like to go alone. Can I?"

"Of course," I said.

She walked to the door, turned before touching the knob, and said, "I have a room in Denver. It's on Colfax. It isn't very clean. It doesn't have any furniture. I left my suitcase and other things there."

"Would you like me to drive you down there? We can pick them up."

"I don't want you to. I'll go down and get them alone if I need them. Please don't worry about it."

Ruth and I watched her out the front window for a while as she walked slowly down the hill, resting a few times to catch her breath before she continued. When she got to the pond, she sat down awkwardly on the bank and began to draw.

"She's going to have that baby soon, Ben. I wish the answering service had let us bring her in earlier."

"If she has it before Tuesday, we'll take her to the emergency room. Let's hope it doesn't come to that. It might help, just in case, if you took her to the hospital and let her see the rooms and babies. I wonder if she has any formal identification in the other suitcase?"

We watched her calmly drawing for a few moments. I thought of her in a small room on Colfax. I remember the first time I saw Colfax. It was that part of a big city everybody likes to pretend doesn't exist—cheap bars, darkened movie houses, and the run-down hotels that go with them. I was somewhat relieved Laurel didn't want me to pick up her things. Just driving there made me nervous. I pictured her sick, forsaken, and dejected in a littered room on Colfax, then looked at her watching the ducks gliding across the surface of the pond, etching lines through the water with their motionless passing. Every so often, she would stare at the mountains for a long time, then shift uncomfortably and return to drawing. The snow from the spring storm had all melted, and the day was warm and beautiful. I thought back to this morning, watching Tiffany and Laurel feeding the duck, coaxing it out from under the car with soggy dog food. They had both laughed, down on their hands and knees peering under the car with their arms outstretched. Every time the duck would snap at the food they would jerk their hands back and giggle, but the duck had tried to fly against the window of the garage, and we had to let it go. To Tiffany's great disappointment, we opened the door and watched it fly out over the lawn and down to the pond.

Ruth had gone upstairs during my reveries and now returned holding some large sheets of paper.

"Look at the colors," she said, holding out three pictures. "She has real talent."

The drawings were all of the mountains. There were soft shadings and bright spring colors. One was of a brook in a flower-covered alpine meadow.

"Did she show you these?"

"Yes, the other day when I went up to get her clothes. She had them spread out on the bed."

"She ought to be in school, Ruth. I wonder if we could get her a scholarship? I know some people in the university's scholarship office."

"Are we being foolish, Ben?"

"What do you mean?"

"We don't even know who she really is. We don't know her first or last name or where she's from. Now we're talking about scholarships. I even called Brother Little about hiring her at his plant, so she could work here in the area."

"You did?"

"Yesterday."

"What did he say?"

"When I told him about her, he said he could find a place for her, one where she wouldn't be threatened, where she could work next to somebody from the stake."

"Did you tell her?"

"Yes. She looked really surprised and said, 'Why would you do that for me?' I said, 'Because we love you, Laurel, and know you're worried about not having a job, and if you want to keep the baby, we don't want that standing in the way.' But then she answered, 'You don't really know me.'"

"How did you answer that?"

"I didn't have time. She went upstairs and shut her door."

"But we *don't* really know her. Maybe we're being foolish, and yet there's no reason why she can't work here. What's wrong with hoping everything will work out right? If only for Chad and Jenni so they can adopt the baby. Who knows—she's asked questions about the Church and about the temple. Why can't she become a member? Things like that happen."

We watched Laurel for a few more moments, both of us lost in making and remaking our plans.

"Ben, why don't you ask her if she'd like to go to the Denver Art Museum? She might really enjoy it."

"Okay, but let's give her a few more minutes alone."

We went to the museum that evening. Laurel wanted to see every painting, every art object, but landscape paintings especially captivated her. She would stand in front of each, asking us if we knew where it was, had we been there, was it in Colorado? Then she'd talk about the colors, which ones she felt were right, which ones she'd change. She didn't like the dark or intense ones. They weren't like nature, she said. When the colors were just right, she called the painting "color-crowned."

We walked through the gallery twice. We were worried about her getting tired, but she sat down every few minutes to rest. She wanted to go through one more time, but we were afraid it would frighten her to walk across a semi-deserted parking lot so late at night. One the way home I asked her where she learned so much about art.

"From pictures," she answered.

"Didn't you ever have any classes?"

"No, I'd look at pictures."

"Not even in high school?"

"I couldn't." She was becoming sullen so I stopped asking questions. I felt I needed to say something to break her mood.

"Ruth showed me your drawings, Laurel—you have talent."

She smiled.

"I like to look at calendars and draw them. I can sit and draw for hours. I love the colors. That's the best part of drawing."

"Would you like to go to school and take classes, Laurel?"

"I never could. It costs too much money."

"You have enough talent I think you could get a scholarship."

She waited for me to say more. When I didn't, she asked, "How do you get them?"

"We could show some of your work to some friends of mine at the university. They would at least tell us your chances."

"But they wouldn't know me."

"We could recommend you, and they know us."

She stared at me a long time without speaking. She had a look on her face as if she wanted to know what I really thought. I became uncomfortable when she didn't look away from my glances.

"It's just a suggestion, Laurel," I finally said. "Think about it and let me know. We'd do all we could to help you get a scholarship if you'd like to take classes."

She turned away and looked out the window and finally closed her eyes. By the time we got home she was asleep again. We helped her into the house, and Ruth helped her into bed. Before Ruth left the room she asked, "Can we go there again?"

"Whenever you want, Laurel. I'm sure Ben would let you come up to the institute and look at the art at the university."

That night I had a dream . . . well, not exactly a dream, more a memory from my childhood that came back while I slept.

I was thirteen, sitting in the bed of an old pickup truck. I had gone with my father to work on the Church welfare farm. We were bumping down the dirt roads. I was cradling the head of a yearling heifer in my arms, pulled up against my lap. She was tied up so she wouldn't kick me. She had thrashed her head so violently when we loaded her in the pickup that my dad was afraid she'd injure herself more. She had pink eye so badly she was blind and was scared from bumping into things. "Climb up there with her, Ben," he had suggested. "Hold her head snug against you so she can't hurt herself. She's afraid, so talk softly to her." I climbed in cautiously and eased into position next to her until I could grab her head firmly. She had fought for a few moments, but eventually settled onto the bed of the truck.

I talked to her all the way. I remember her eyes ringed with infection, the deep brown, almost black orbs staring at me without blinking—as though with effort, she could penetrate the blindness, let the light in, and know the voice that spoke.

When we got down the canyon, we drove into the middle of the corral and as gently as we could, let her down and untied the ropes. My dad told me to climb the fence because he didn't know what she would do when she was free. The other boys and I were on the fence when we untied the last loops of the rope. She leaped up and ran, banging into the cedar poles before she stopped and shook off the blow. Dad yelled at us to get completely off the fence as he was afraid she might knock us off if she hit it again where we were. She turned toward the sound of his voice, lowered her head, and charged him. He jumped back into the bed of the pickup. She kept coming. We all yelled, but couldn't stop her. I shut my eyes at the last second, but I heard her head hit the trailer hitch full force and drop to the ground. She died instantly. I had cried. I felt ashamed then and hid behind the barn, because she was only a range cow. But I could see her eyes, the fear, and knew I hadn't stopped it when I held her head in the back of the truck. Dad found me and took me home.

I didn't tell Ruth about my memory even though I wanted to. I looked at Laurel the next morning while we ate breakfast trying to see her eyes. When she looked at me there was no terror, no hint of fear, just a mild look as if I had not answered all her questions.

# Chapter 9

It was Sunday, so after breakfast we dressed the kids for church and Laurel went back to her room to dress. There were a few anxious moments when everyone was ready to go and her door had not yet opened. Ruth knocked and softly said, "Laurel, we're ready."

The door opened and Laurel walked out. She had on her new dress, her hair combed down, and she had put her new shoes on. Everything fit perfectly. She stood shyly at the top of the stairs for a few moments looking down at us.

"You look lovely, Laurel," I said. "Everyone at church will be delighted to meet you."

She looked a little nervous.

"How many are there?"

"Oh, you don't have to meet them all, but Mormons can be very friendly sometimes. Don't be nervous."

"I'll stay right with you, Laurel," my wife assured her. "And we have a meeting just for the women. Sometimes we talk about literature, music, and art. Maybe you could come and talk about painting like you did at the museum."

"What will they think . . . ?" Laurel hesitated.

"Oh, don't worry about that. They won't think anything." Then she chuckled. "Besides, Mormon women are nearly always pregnant."

We drove to the chapel, the kids practicing their Primary songs as we went. When we got to the chapel Laurel was a little hesitant about entering, but the kids pulled her along. Once inside, so many of the members came to talk to Ruth or to meet Laurel that there was no time for her to consider what was happening.

During the meeting Laurel had lots of questions. She asked me most of them because I was still the reverend to her. She wondered why I wasn't up front. The children were sitting in the choir seats for their program. All three of mine waved to her during their song. She waved back enthusiastically the first time, then realized what she had done and pulled her hand down. I told her it didn't matter—parents always got carried away when their children went to the front of the chapel.

She asked questions about the sacrament and sat stone silent during it. After the meeting, we took her to a small Sunday School class because it was less threatening.

She also met the missionaries assigned to our ward. I explained who they were and what they did, adding that I had done the same thing in Europe. That fascinated her.

"That's why you're a reverend," she said with delight.

Ruth took Laurel with her to Relief Society while I went to priesthood meeting. At the end of priesthood, while waiting in the foyer, a member drew me aside.

"Don't you have to be careful about transients like her?"

"Why?" I asked.

"She came from Pearl Street, didn't she?"

"She's from the East," I answered.

"A lot of them come from there. Boulder attracts them. You weren't here in the late sixties when they overran the campus and town."

"Laurel's different." I was getting a bit sharp.

"Please don't take offense, Ben. I know you have to deal with them more than we do, but sometimes these people con you. They play on your sympathy. After they get what they want from you, they take off."

"I appreciate your concern, but Laurel wouldn't do that."

"You can't always tell."

"We've had Laurel with us for a week. She's not after anything."

I turned away before I could say anything I would later regret, more bothered by the conversation than I knew I should be. I saw Tiffany and Bethany coming out of their classes. We walked together and found Ruth and Laurel, then Joseph, and went home and ate dinner.

The day couldn't have gone better, I thought. Laurel sat and paged through the Book of Mormon she had received at church. Tiffany sat next to her with Bethany and told her about the pictures. Later Laurel took Tiffany down to the pond with her and let her watch while she drew. They stayed down there about two hours until it started to get cool. When they got back to the house, I asked to see what she was doing.

"It's not finished," she said as she went upstairs to put her things away, then came back downstairs and sat with Tiffany at the piano.

"I'll play a song, Tiffany."

While she was playing, Ruth came in from the kitchen and

stood next to me. I don't think Laurel knew we were there. It was the same song she always played, the wistful melancholy notes.

She hummed the melody. Ruth and I started to turn away when we heard words mixed occasionally with the humming. They grew more frequent. Her voice was high and tight, almost forced, and she sang with her eyes closed.

The song told a story of a man walking with his daughter through a meadow near a stream. They never talked, just walked, until she stopped and picked a flower. One by one she pulled the petals off until she came to the last petal. She looked up and the man, far in the distance, was still walking.

Laurel sang the song over and over, and the little girl would pick the flower, and the father would keep on walking.

Tiffany finally got bored. She slipped from the bench and ran off. Laurel kept singing. Ruth and I didn't watch the clock, but the room grew dark as the sun set, and Ruth had to turn the light on by the piano. Laurel stopped. She turned and looked at Ruth, smiled and said, "I'm tired. I'll go to bed now. You don't need to wait."

# Chapter 10

*I* had planned to go to work late that Monday, because Brother Curtis was coming. After his visit, Ruth was going to take Laurel to the hospital. Since the hospital was in Boulder, I planned to go to the institute from there. While waiting for Brother Curtis, I got a phone call from Karen.

"There's a young man here who I think you'd like to talk to. He's the one who left a few of his books."

"Put him on, Karen."

A few seconds later I heard Adam's voice through the receiver.

"How are you, Adam?"

"Fine."

"Are you settled?"

"Not really. I wanted to use a few of my books . . ."

"Whatever you want, Adam. I'll be up in a little while; we'll go through them. I'm afraid we may have lent some."

"I can come back later."

"Why don't you wait till I come. Do you have any pressing plans for the day?"

"Not really, but I feel stupid sitting around here. Are you coming up soon?"

I struggled with the decision. Brother Curtis would be there in a few minutes, yet there was a need in Adam's voice.

"I may be a while. I've got somebody here. I believe it was you who sent her to us."

"The girl that's going to have a baby, the timid one?"

"Yes, she's been staying with us. We have a man from LDS Social Services coming this morning."

"I'm sorry to bother you. You need to be home."

"Adam, how did you meet her?"

"I just met her at the mall. She was desperate. I could see she was confused. She was afraid of everyone."

"Why did you give her the institute address?"

"Well, I figured you could maybe do something for her, maybe she wouldn't be afraid of you."

"Do you know anything about her?"

The doorbell rang. It was Brother Curtis. Adam heard it through the phone. Ruth opened the door and greeted him.

"You need to go."

"Listen, Adam, I'd really like to talk with you. Will you come back later?"

There was a pause.

"I'll come up to the institute now if you want me to. My wife can handle things here."

"No, you need to be there. That girl needs you more. I'm okay. I just needed a book or two."

"Adam, will you come back?"

I could hear the phone's hum as I waited for his answer.

"Things aren't working out here in Boulder."

"Does that mean you're going again?"

I could hear my wife and Brother Curtis talking in the background while I waited for an answer.

"Adam, are you leaving?"

"Brother Christianson, could I see you?"

"I'll be right up."

"No, you stay and help her. You need to do that. I'll wait."

"I can come . . ."

"I'll wait. You don't need to worry I'll skip out again."

I turned and waved to Brother Curtis who was standing in the hallway entry still talking with Ruth.

"Adam, are you all right?"

There was a long pause.

"I just talked to someone on the phone. It rattled me a bit, that's all. I'm fine."

"I'll be up in an hour, but if I need to come right now, Ruth can . . ."

"I'll wait. Do you think you could let me sit in your office though instead of the lounge?"

"Sure, I'll tell Karen to open the door and let you sit down."

"Yeah, okay."

I talked to Karen again, told her to open the office, and then hung up.

Brother Curtis held out his hand to me and shook it firmly. I knew as I saw him the second time that Laurel was going to have trouble talking to him. Though he was good-looking, stocky with dark brown hair, he was tall and wore dark glasses that partially concealed his eyes.

"Laurel is down by the pond."

"I know. Your wife showed me. Does she go there often?"

"Several times a day."

"Maybe it would be a good place to talk with her. Why don't you go down and ask her."

"Before we do that, have you heard any . . ."

"Any word on your cousin and his wife? Yes. They've been approved. I've checked with Interstate Compact. Everything can be arranged."

"Do they know—my cousin, I mean?"

"Not many details. They know there is a strong possibility they will have a baby within a few weeks. They're very excited, but we still need to talk with Laurel."

"Okay, I'll go talk with her. She was a little nervous this morning. I think that's why she went to the pond."

Ruth and I walked down the slope.

"That was Adam on the phone, wasn't it?"

"I didn't want to worry you with Brother Curtis here for the interview."

"But it worried you, didn't it?"

"Yes. He wants to talk. I think he's getting ready to take off again."

"Then you need to go now. We'll be all right."

"I can't. How would it look to Laurel—especially now with Brother Curtis here. Adam said he'd wait. I believe this time he meant it."

We walked in silence a few steps. Ruth took my hand and said, "I guess he came back at the wrong time for you. I'm sorry."

"Laurel's just as important as he is, but I feel torn. Will Laurel notice it?"

"I don't think so. She's been so worried about this interview."

"I think he wants to tell me what he's done."

"Maybe that's what he needs. It will help him. It helped Laurel that night to tell us."

"Did it really? Sometimes I look at her and I don't think we've helped her at all. She doesn't seem to be changing. She's less terrified, that's all."

"Maybe the changes won't be ones you can see right away."

We were almost down the hill. Laurel's back was to us. She wasn't drawing anymore. Her head was down, studying her palms.

"What if I can't help him? What if I don't know what to say? I'm no bishop, Ruth."

"No, but he trusts you. And if he needs to tell you, you'll listen and know what to do."

"But I don't want to hear it. I don't know why, but I'm afraid."

We reached Laurel. She didn't turn around when we came up to her. We sat on either side.

"Laurel," Ruth started, "Brother Curtis is here from the Church."

"I know."

"He's the nicest man."

"Will I have to tell him about why I'm going to have a baby?"

Her voice was regaining the fear and tension of those first days.

"You don't have to tell him anything, just listen. You don't have to even talk if you don't want to. He told me that."

"He'll ask about the baby."

"He just wants to know about finding it a good home, if that's what you still want."

"I'm not married. There would be no daddy. Do I have to talk to him?"

She looked down into her lap. She had turned her drawing over. My eyes followed her gaze to where she was turning a blue chalk over and over again in her fingers, rubbing it into her palms. Ruth placed her hand on her shoulder, looking into her eyes.

"Laurel. Would you like to talk with Brother Curtis here? You don't have to come up to the house if you don't want to. You can talk to him here in the open."

"I'll come to the house," she said. "I don't want him to come here."

She tried to get up. It was difficult, so we helped her. I wondered how much longer the baby would wait and if Laurel had had any other pains.

As we walked up to the house, I pictured Adam sitting nervously in my chair. I wondered how long he would stay or if he'd already left. Then I wondered if we were going to have more trouble with Laurel. She had been so good the last few days. When we got to the door, she stopped, frightened once again.

"I want to go to my room first."

"Would you just like to meet him?" I suggested.

"I want to go to my room. Please."

"Okay, Laurel. We'll go right in."

We opened the door. Brother Curtis remained sitting on the couch because I had warned him his height might frighten her.

"Hello, Laurel," he greeted her.

She didn't look at him but kept her head down and climbed the stairs with Ruth. I went over to Brother Curtis.

"She wanted to go to her room first," I explained.

"She won't see me," he said. "I've seen this before."

"What should we do?"

"Tell her she can stay in her room. I'll pull a chair up outside the door with my back to her. Then she can look out if she wants to. You can go into the room with her and your wife."

I went upstairs and knocked at the door.

"No!" Laurel's voice came back.

"It's me, Laurel. Brother Curtis knows you're afraid of him, that you don't know him. He understands. He's not angry. He said you can stay in your room with Ruth and me if you want. He'll sit here by the stairs, and you can listen to him through the door."

There was no reply. I went down to the kitchen and brought up a chair and set it at the top of the stairs about three feet from the door. Brother Curtis sat down while I sat on the top step. Laurel opened the door a few inches and peeked out.

"Laurel," he started. "I know this is hard for you. Maybe someday if we become friends, we can talk about your feelings. We won't talk about that today. We'll just talk about the baby. Will that be too hard?"

I watched her, still peeking through the door glancing down the stairs every few minutes.

"No," she finally answered.

"Brother and Sister Christianson have told me that you want the baby to have a home where there will be a good father and mother. We've found a home like that—a couple who haven't been able to have children, who want a child dearly."

"Will they treat the baby nice?"

"I know they will. They are members of our church. I can't tell you much more about them. We've learned that it's best that way. You'll have to trust us that the baby will have a fine home. I can only promise you that it will. People who want children that much are good parents."

Laurel opened the door a little wider.

"What do I have to do?"

"I'll explain what the laws of Colorado and the nation

require. You stop me anytime you have a question. Will you stop me if you have a question?"

"Yes."

"There are some papers you need to sign after the baby's born. We can't really do anything until that time."

"What papers?"

"They're not very pleasant sounding papers. They're called 'Relinquishment of Parental Rights.' They say that you give all rights to your baby to LDS Social Services. That means you let us find the future home for your baby. I'll leave a copy of them here if you'd like to see what they are and talk to the Christiansons about them. If you have questions, you can call me on the phone or have the Christiansons call."

"Is that all I have to do?"

"I wish that was all, Laurel, but for the protection of you and the baby and in some cases the father . . ."

"There isn't a father!"

I watched her hand try to twist the wood of the door.

"I understand, Laurel. Please don't worry. Let me explain. After the baby is born we will need to go to the courthouse and see a judge."

"No! I don't want to see anyone. How come I have to keep seeing new people and telling them?"

"The judge is a very kind man. He's over sixty."

"I don't want to see him."

"He just needs to ask you some questions, Laurel."

"Everyone asks . . ."

"I understand how you feel. Please, let me finish. May I finish?"

"Yes."

I saw Ruth standing behind Laurel; she started rubbing Laurel's shoulders.

"The judge just wants to ask you if you really want to give up your baby. He needs to know that you're not just doing it because you don't have enough money or because we're forcing you. He wants to make sure what we're planning is the best for you and the baby."

"You can tell him it's what I want. I don't want to see anybody else."

I noticed the door was closing more. The look of being trapped filtered back into her face and eyes.

"Laurel, I wish I could do that for you. I would if the law would let me, but the law won't. It makes us see the judge, but it doesn't take very long—only a few minutes."

"I don't want to. Please don't make me. Ruth, don't let him make me."

Her voice was back to the first day I met her. Brother Curtis realized he was pushing her and decided to change the subject, letting us ease her into the idea of seeing the judge when we were alone with her.

"We'll wait on the judge for now, Laurel. You think about it. But there is one other thing *I* need to do, Laurel, for us to receive the baby. I have to put a small note in the newspaper announcing the hearing date."

"Why?" Laurel asked.

Brother Curtis looked at me and hesitated.

"The law requires it to protect the father's rights, but in this case . . ."

"No! There wasn't a father. Please! No, you can't do that!"

"I know how you feel, Laurel. It's just a formality."

Laurel shut the door. I heard her voice talking to Ruth.

"I don't want to talk anymore. I want him to go."

Brother Curtis looked at me with pain in his eyes.

"I'm sorry, Brother Christianson."

"We'll explain things to her. She'll be all right. I've seen her this way before. She'll cry for a while, then she'll be normal again. It's getting better."

"I'd better go then. Please let me know. I can come back anytime, and we'll try again."

"Maybe when the baby is born, she won't feel so desperate anymore."

"I'll leave the papers. Maybe they'll help."

I showed him to the door, then looked at the papers in my hand and read the words that were so unsettling: Relinquishment of Parental Rights.

# Chapter 11

*I* went upstairs to help Ruth for a moment.

"We'll be all right, Ben," she said. "You hurry up to the institute. Go on! I'll be fine."

She turned to Laurel, smoothed her hair a bit and said, "We're going to the hospital to see the maternity ward and the little babies, aren't we, Laurel?"

She nodded her head and smiled a tiny smile.

"You're sure you'll be all right? I may be a while."

"We'll be just fine."

All the way to Boulder I felt anxious about Adam. I wished the interview with Laurel had gone better. I would have been calmer, but it troubled me that she wouldn't talk to Brother Curtis. I wondered if Adam had really waited like he said or if the office was now empty. What could we have done differently? I tried to put my fears and what had just happened behind me and prepare my mind for Adam if he was still in the office, but Laurel's night of terror was lighted again in my mind, and I could feel the resentment and hatred toward her tormentors rising hot all around me. And if Adam was gone, what would I have to put those fires out?

I was feeling that resentment when I walked into the institute and saw Adam sitting in a chair through the open door of my office. He had one of the janitor's children on his lap. He was drawing pictures for her. When he saw me, he jumped up immediately, gave the drawing to the child, and circled to the front of the desk. We shook hands awkwardly without speaking. I sat down in one of the office chairs in front of the desk. Adam remained standing.

"Hello, Adam. Sit down, please."

He hadn't changed much. His hair was a bit longer, but his clothes looked new and clean. He looked directly at me, searching my face for a moment. I tried to drain the anxiety out of it and searched his own, trying to bring back all my experiences with him, wishing I had kept my notes and had searched them before this meeting. He finally sat down and turned his gaze from my face.

"It's wonderful to see you again. Did you find the books you wanted?"

"Yes. I looked up a few things."

"You can stay for a while, can't you?"

He sat on the edge of the chair and leaned forward on his knees, looking at me once more intently. I could hear the silence and felt nervous.

"I'm sorry I didn't get up sooner. I'd have come, you know."

"I didn't mind waiting."

He was still looking at me. I looked at his hands tight on his knees.

"You mentioned a phone call. I . . ."

"It was nothing. How's the girl?"

He didn't want to talk about it, so I let him change the subject.

"I wish I could say it went well, but it didn't. There's a lot of damage in her life. Sometimes I despair because I don't know if anything or anyone can straighten it all out again."

"Was it a boyfriend?" He looked down at his feet, then back into my face.

"She was assaulted by two men." There was a barb of anger in my voice. I tried to keep it out, but it was too near to me. I still couldn't say the word. It seemed to hang in my throat and pinch my mouth shut. He studied my eyes again, then looked past me to the wall.

"Did they ever find them?"

"No, she never told. They got away."

"Maybe she could . . ."

"She'll never tell. They'll never be caught."

He looked out the door. It gave me a chance to study his face without his eyes searching for something in my own. He got up slowly and closed the door, then sat down again, still leaning over his knees.

"Brother Christianson, what do you think of those men?"

I didn't answer right away. I tried to see through the question. It was the kind I would have written down and thought about later. I finally asked him, "Why do you ask me that question, Adam? I don't know how to answer you."

"I want to know how you really feel, not what you think an institute director should answer or what he thinks I want to hear."

"Why is it so important?" I tried to stall so I could think.

"I want to know the truth. What you as a person think."

"All right, Adam. I suppose the feelings I have inside me

would be close to hatred. They're strong feelings, so strong that sometimes they take away the sorrow I feel when I think of Laurel."

He accepted my answer, but I sensed that I hadn't said the right thing. He sat quietly as if the conversation was over. I had to say more.

"For some reason, Adam, I feel like I have to justify those feelings."

"No, not to me."

"I want to try. I don't like to admit that I have those emotions. I wish I didn't. It's just that I've never seen anyone suffer so much before, especially someone who did nothing to deserve it. She's like a child. She's defenseless and always will be. I don't know why she's that way, but as long as I live I will never forget hearing her the night she told us what happened. It was as though she were reliving it again as she must have relived it over and over in her mind until it has made her afraid of everyone and everything. It's like those two men even now, far away, still have the power to hurt her."

"Do you think God hates people who hurt other people like they did to her?"

I thought I saw the reason for his question and answered carefully.

"I don't think God hates anyone."

"Ignores them then?"

"I don't know how He feels, Adam. I know how I feel. I can't comprehend Him, but I believe He still loves them."

There wasn't a deep conviction in my voice. He looked into my face again, then rubbed his hands over his face and dropped his head.

"Adam," I said softly. "I want to talk about you."

"You are."

"Not really. I know God loves you. I believe . . ."

"Would you want to help those two men?"

"You're not those two men. You haven't done what they've done."

"I know, but you don't know what I've done. What if I caused as much damage to other people as they did to her?"

He pushed his fingers against his head. The skin of his temple was white from the pressure.

"Willingly, Adam, or in weakness? By mistake or by accident? I can't believe . . ."

"If I did it, it was willful."

He said the words loudly with more emotion than any I had heard him speak. I waited a few moments for the emotion to drain from the room.

"I don't know those men. I know you. I know . . ."

"You don't know me. Maybe that's why I don't tell you. Why I won't tell you. But I had to come in and talk to you. I can't tell you, Brother Christianson. I don't want to see that look on your face. You will never understand what it's like to be on my side. It's like standing on the edge of a lake trying to talk to somebody on the distant side. They only hear you if they listen. But they never listen hard enough, they always want to talk, trying to make *you* listen. You're not talking to them, and they're not talking to you. I said, 'I'm sorry!' I said, 'I did what I did. I'm sorry somebody else got hurt. I didn't want it that way. I was weak. I was rebellious. I made a mistake. I . . . I sinned!' They say all the right words—they understand, they forgive: 'God loves you,' and all that. But their faces keep shouting, 'Somebody got hurt, somebody who didn't deserve it!' You can always hear it in their voices. And if it isn't there, you put it there yourself, because you've been shouting at yourself right along with them from the start. Then God shouts it because your guilt says the same thing to you when you try to pray."

He stopped. He was breathing heavily. I watched him trying to regain control. I had never heard him say so much at one time in all our conversations.

"Adam, was it the phone call?"

"No, it's nothing . . ."

"Someone said something to you, someone from . . ."

"Brother Christianson, will you please listen to me, just listen?"

There was no anger in his voice, no frustration, just a plea.

"I'm sorry, Adam, I'll try to listen."

"I don't want to tell you what I did because with you I feel the love and hurt for me, not pity, but the understanding that doesn't condemn, just loves and hurts and wants to give. I've seen that in your eyes for me. I hear it in your voice. But when you start probing, I . . . Don't make me tell you. I want to tell you, but I'm afraid."

He dropped his head into his hands again, his elbows pressing into his knees.

"Oh, Adam."

"Why doesn't God hear me? Why does my own voice shout back louder than all the rest?"

His voice began to break, and his fingers grasped his knees to stop the trembling. I stared at his hands, wanting them to relax.

"I don't understand all that God feels or why He does what He does, but I believe He never leaves the lake, that He doesn't shout across it when you want Him to listen. Maybe it's time for you to stop shouting at yourself and listen. Have you listened?"

"I'm afraid. I'm afraid to listen, to tell you. I'm afraid the look will leave you, and you'll shout it too with your eyes and your voice like you shout it with those two men."

"They did a terrible thing, Adam. Don't ask me to forgive them, to stop shouting at them with all that I am, 'You've committed a horrible crime! You've destroyed a human life!' I can't, Adam, I can't. I'd lie to you if I could. I'd . . ."

"Help me, Brother Christianson! I can't see God's face, only yours."

His voice failed him; he fought for control, but his tears were falling.

"How can I help you? What can I say to make you believe there's hope?"

"I don't know. I've hurt people I love."

He didn't look up this time. I waited for him to, but he wouldn't. I waited for the right words to come, wanted to hear my own voice speak them, but they didn't come. Finally I said, "I'll give you all I have. I won't probe. Don't tell me what happened. I'll feel the love and grief for you. I do feel it. Maybe more for you than for Laurel, but not for the two men, Adam, not for them. For your sake I want to. Maybe to love and hurt, we need to see in their faces what I see in yours. It's all I can give."

"I need to go now."

"Please don't. I want to . . ."

"I only wanted you to know so you won't think you've failed me."

"But I have."

"No. You don't understand, but you haven't failed."

"Can't you go home? Your mother and father must love and hurt for you."

"Not yet."

"Why? . . . I'm sorry, I didn't mean to ask that."

"They can't help me."

"Nor I?"

"Not anymore. You gave me all you could, all I wanted."

"And God?"

"I don't know."

I watched him walk across campus back toward Pearl Street and knew somehow I wouldn't see him again. I understood, for the first time in my life as I watched him disappear on the campus, a scripture I had always puzzled over, a definition of Godhood given by God Himself, describing it as a "far more and an exceeding and an eternal weight of glory," and I knew it was more than creating worlds and speaking to prophets. God watched Laurel and two men next to a burnt-out streetlamp and wept for all, though I could not.

# Chapter 12

I walked across the street to the campus and down to Old Main, then to the turtle ponds. I stayed there, thinking about Laurel and Adam. When the sun set and the campus faded into the shadows of the arching trees, there was no anger, just grief.

When I got home, Laurel was resting in bed. The trip to the hospital had been good for her. I wanted to talk about Adam, but waited while Ruth told me about the hospital.

"She stood in front of the nursery glass for the longest time and stared at the babies. I think it eased a little of the pressure to see the labor room. But she still doesn't want to see a judge and have a notice in the paper. She talked about it all day long."

"Well, let's not worry about it now. It seems like every time we try to help, we end up putting her through more agony. What's going to happen tomorrow when she sees the doctor?"

"That's the one thing she needs to do, and soon. She had some pains again this afternoon. She tried to hide it, but she went right upstairs when we got home and laid down. I told the kids to be quiet so she could rest. She's still upstairs. The kids are in the basement."

"It hasn't been really fair for them, has it?"

I couldn't hide my depression from Ruth; she had sensed it from the beginning.

"Ben," she asked. "It went badly with Adam, didn't it?"

"Not so badly, I guess. At least he talked, maybe that's something, like you said."

"Is he coming back?"

"No, I guess I failed. I didn't know what to say. I didn't know how to help him. I wanted to tell him about forgiveness and love, but I never really had the chance."

"I'm sorry. It must be terrible for him."

"You know, Ruth, I don't even know what he did."

"Would it make any difference if you did?"

"I would hope not. I wouldn't have thought so before I met Laurel, but now, maybe it would. What does that say about me?"

"Only that you're human."

I thought about her response, then turned and stared out the window.

"I don't know, Ruth. I'm glad I still don't know. I could have . . . if I had pushed, I believe he would have told me. Maybe I should have."

I could see the pond. There was a faint reflection of the mountains on its surface. "I'm glad I don't know, not for Adam's sake, but for my own. Perhaps knowing would have made the difference he feared." I turned and faced her again. "I wouldn't have wanted it to, but if it had, I don't think I want to know that about myself. Maybe I'm inwardly relieved he's gone again."

She studied my face for several moments, then kissed me lightly on the cheek.

"You're wrong, Ben Christianson. I think you would have risked everything if you could have helped him. And you're not relieved. You weren't the first time he left, and this time it's harder on you because it didn't turn out the way you wanted it to, the way you felt it should have. You don't believe he'll ever come back, do you?"

"No, but I can't admit that to myself. I can't let the hope die."

✦ ✦ ✦

In the morning, Laurel stayed in bed. Ruth took her up a glass of orange juice. When she came back down, I asked her if I should stay home, but she said to go on to work.

"You've already cancelled an afternoon meeting so you can go with us to the doctor." As I was going out the door, Laurel came out of the bedroom. She looked tired and tense. She had her sketchbook under her arm.

"I'm going down to the pond."

I helped her out the door and watched her move heavily down the hill, then got in the car and drove to Boulder. I felt an uneasiness all morning. Brother Curtis called and asked how she was doing. He said everything could be ready for the adoption as soon as the baby was born. He cautioned me about contacting my cousin and especially about telling him I knew the mother. He sighed and said it would be necessary for Laurel to see the judge. He said he'd try to talk to the judge before so he would understand her anxieties and make the interview as gentle and quick as possible. There was even a chance the judge could come and talk to her in the hospital, if the courthouse frightened her. I told him I understood and then said it might be best for us to wait until the baby was born.

"We're taking her to see the doctor this afternoon. We're

hoping it will be positive for her. Perhaps that will make your job easier, too."

"Please let me know how it turns out. I'll be praying for you."

He hung up and I tried once again to get involved in a lesson preparation. Adam kept returning to my mind like a nagging ache. Ruth had been right. At ten o'clock, Karen came into my office.

"There's a President Ellis from Arizona on the phone. He got your letter about Adam. He wants to talk to you."

She crossed her fingers and smiled while I picked up the phone, then closed the door so I'd have some privacy.

"Hello, this is Brother Ellis from Phoenix. I received your letter today. We had a boy about a year and a half ago that ran away. He fits the description in your letter. His parents are very worried about him. Before I telephone them, I want to make sure that your young man is their son. I don't want to add to their anxieties."

"I hope I can help, President. I'll do all I can, but it may be too late."

"Oh? Why is that?"

"I don't think he'll come in to see me again, and he never would tell me where he was living or where he was going."

We talked about Adam and by the end of the conversation we were certain he was the same boy. His real name was Jeff Thomas.

"President, I got the impression from Adam that he was afraid to go home, but from what you've told me, his parents are really worried."

"There are some problems with his parents. He's caused a great deal of anguish for his family. Did he ever talk to you about it?"

"Not in detail. I know something happened that he feels

guilty about. I'd rather you not tell me, though. Our relationship is based on my lack of that knowledge. I don't think I'll see him again, but if he came back once, I don't want him to notice a change."

"I'm not sure I understand what you're talking about."

"It's just something he said. Tell his parents he's still struggling to forgive himself, and he appears to be well."

"That will be some comfort to them. I'm sure they would like to talk to you, if you wouldn't mind."

"If you give me their address, I'd like to write them a letter. I know it sounds cruel, but I'd rather write the letter first. I'd have a hard time explaining some things over the phone."

He gave me their address, expressed gratitude for my time and expense, and was about to hang up, when I stopped him.

"President—one more thing, please?"

"Yes?"

"The damage? Just in case I see him again, is it irreparable or has Adam . . . has Jed taken too great a burden on himself?"

"There isn't much hope that what's been done can be repaired. Do you want me to tell you? You seem to be closer to him than any of us here have achieved. You might be able to help him if you know the details. I don't believe we'd be breaking confidences."

I thought for a few moments and saw Adam's fingers pushed into his temples again, then him standing on the shore of a lake, alone and yelling across the solitude.

"No, President—thank you for the offer, but I need to leave our relationship as it is. I hope I haven't learned too much already."

I left the office and drove home. Ruth, Laurel, and the boys were eating lunch. Laurel had her new clothes on but had put her hair back up in a bun on the top of her head. I had almost forgotten she used to wear it that way.

An hour later we were in front of the clinic. We went inside and sat in the waiting room. Ruth was holding Laurel's hand, telling her there was nothing to worry about. The nurse came in a few minutes later.

"Mrs. Christianson, you can bring her in now."

We all stood up.

"I'm sorry, Mr. Christianson, but you'll have to wait here."

"Of course," I said, but Laurel wouldn't go.

"I want the reverend to come, too."

"He can't. I'm sorry," said the nurse. "The doctor can't examine you with him there. Mrs. Christianson can come, though."

"The doctor was only going to ask me questions," Laurel said looking at Ruth.

"He won't do anything you don't want, Laurel. Come in with me, please. It's going to be all right."

"I'll wait right here, Laurel. Go on in with Ruth. She'll watch you."

The room was suddenly too quiet. Silently I prayed, "Please, Father, she's got to see the doctor."

"If you'll come with me," the nurse continued.

Ruth tugged gently at Laurel's arm, and they disappeared into the back rooms. I waited for about five minutes, trying to get interested in the month-old magazines. It was no use. I kept straining to hear any sounds coming from the back rooms.

Suddenly voices came from the back. Then Laurel came running through the door with Ruth and the nurse behind her. Laurel rushed to the front door, opened it and ran out into the parking lot.

"I'm sorry," the nurse kept saying. "I didn't know she was so sensitive."

"What happened, Ruth?" I said as we both went out the door, following Laurel. She was about fifty feet into the parking lot and still running. Ruth pulled at my arm and stopped me.

"Sooner or later we need to stop chasing her. Let her go. She needs to come back on her own."

"What if she doesn't?"

"We'll have to take that chance. Maybe Sister Hancock was right that first night. We've hovered over her too much."

Laurel had crossed the parking lot now and was disappearing down the walk. She was no longer running. We watched her become smaller and smaller.

"What happened, Ruth?" I said again.

"The doctor insisted that the nurse get her into a gown so he could examine her."

"I thought he understood."

"I was sure I spelled it out firmly enough when I talked to him on the phone. I guess he didn't realize how serious a problem we had in bringing her to him."

"She panicked?"

"Things just got out of control. The doctor came into the room again to see what the matter was. That's when she ran."

"What are we going to do now?"

"I guess we wait here and hope."

We sat in the car for over an hour trying to talk. It was no good. After fifteen more minutes, I was ready to go home when Laurel came back around the corner and walked to the car. Her head was down, and she was crying.

"I was bad, I know. I saw you waiting for me. Can't we just let the baby come? Then I will hurt so bad I won't care."

Ruth sighed.

"I guess we'll have to, Laurel. Do you want to get in, and we'll take you home?"

"Could we go back to the art museum instead? Just for a little while?"

"The girls will be coming home from school in about half an hour, Laurel; somebody needs to be there to meet them and take care of the boys," Ruth said. There was a change in her tone, not very noticeable, just a hint of exhaustion, I thought.

"I'll meet them, Ruth. You take Laurel down to the art museum."

Ruth dropped me off at home, then went to the museum. They stayed until it closed and got home just before nine o'clock. Ruth said Laurel had been as thrilled as she had the first visit. Laurel ate a little dinner. She looked more tired than I had seen her in days. She wouldn't talk to anyone after eating, just went into the living room and played the wistful little song on the piano, no words, no humming. Something wasn't right, I felt it. Ruth seemed different, too. I excused it as the mess at the doctor's office. I figured we would probably be going to the hospital that night. Laurel went to her room early. A few minutes later Ruth said, "I'm really tired tonight. I think I'll go to bed early, too." I checked on her a little later. The light in our room was off. It was then I noticed the light still coming from under the door to Laurel's room. I started to call to her, changed my mind and watched some television for a few hours. At eleven-thirty I finally felt tired enough to sleep and climbed the stairs. Laurel's light was still on.

"Laurel, are you all right?" I whispered through the door.

"I'm fine. I'm drawing." There was a long pause then. "Thank you for waiting."

"What did you say?"

There was no answer. I listened intently and could hear the pastels sliding softly over the paper.

"Laurel, everything is going to be all right. What happened today isn't important."

There was still no answer, just the pastels easing colors across the paper.

"Don't stay up too late, Laurel. You need to rest. The baby isn't going to wait much longer."

"I'm drawing."

"Goodnight, Laurel."

"Goodnight."

Early the next morning I heard her moving around in her room. I glanced at the clock. It was five-fifteen, and the light was just beginning to grey the room into dawn.

She was moving quietly in the room, then her door opened softly with the deliberate ease which told me she was trying to be careful.

She tiptoed down the stairs into the front room. I thought, "I won't get out of bed because she's just going down to the pond to catch the morning colors or go out for a walk."

After a few seconds I eased out of bed and walked silently to the window. Laurel was standing on the sidewalk looking back at the house. Her hair was tied up tightly in the bun on top of her head. She had on the same clothes that she had the first day I saw her sleeping in the Institute lounge. The heavy cloth bag, bulging with her belongings, was hanging from her fingers. She had to hold it with both hands. When she saw me standing at the window, she put her head down, turned to look at the pond, then walked down the sidewalk.

There is a point within all of us when we realize there is

absolutely nothing we can do. We do not understand all the reasons, but we recognize the moment of futility when hope dies. Perhaps someone can understand how I stood and watched Laurel walk down the sidewalk. The sun lifted above the horizon and flooded the room with sunlight. I dressed quietly, trying not to wake Ruth. She opened her eyes, though, and saw me buttoning my shirt and pulling on a pair of moccasins.

"Where are you going so early in the morning?"

"I couldn't sleep very well last night. I'm just going out for a little walk."

"Be careful not to wake Laurel when you go downstairs. I'll have breakfast started in half an hour."

I closed the front door and walked down the sidewalk. I knew where Laurel was going. Just around the corner was a bus stop. When I turned that corner, she was standing there, the bag still dangling from her fingers because she was afraid to put it down. She didn't move or say anything when I walked up to her, nor did I for a few minutes. For once I wanted her to talk first. She stared straight ahead without looking at me.

"I need to leave," she said softly.

"Like this, Laurel?"

"You wouldn't have let me any other way."

"We always told you we wouldn't make you do anything, we wouldn't force you to stay. We didn't yesterday."

"There are other ways of making people stay."

"How, Laurel? Will you help me understand, for Ruth's sake?"

"I'm not worried about Ruth. Ruth is stronger than you. You won't be able to accept this."

"Then help me."

"People have loved you all your life. You know how to feel it and give it back. I can't give it back."

"You don't need to. We never expected it."

"I wanted it. You did, too. There's something wrong with me."

"No, there isn't, Laurel. Love can be learned."

"I can't. I don't know how."

"Won't you please let us teach you?"

"Isn't that what you've been trying to do these last days?"

I stared at the pavement and the shadow of the cloth bag dangling from her hands.

"Laurel, there's going to be another life involved in a few days."

"I won't think about that. I can't think about it—won't you understand?"

"You have to think about it."

"I didn't ask for this life to come. I'm not responsible."

"But it will come just the same; somebody will have to be responsible."

"I won't have to decide anything. They'll come and do what they need to. It won't matter then what I want or do. It won't matter because they will decide everything, and they won't feel anything for me like you do."

"Laurel, we love you."

"I know."

"We want you to stay."

She shifted the bag in her hands. Her fingers held the cloth straps calmly, then she looked at me. There was more I should have said and maybe could have, but the feeling of calm futility was back. It was almost a relief to see the bus round the corner and stop. She climbed the first few steps, then without looking at me, said, "Can I keep the name? It's prettier."

I didn't answer. She climbed the last few steps, stared at the bus driver, then walked past him to the back and sat down.

"I'll pay her fare," I said.

I dug into my pants pocket and found some loose change. I gave him all of it. He dropped it in the machine and closed the door. I stood there and watched him pull the bus away from the curb and then I walked home, wondering how long the calm would last.

I was a few minutes too late. Ruth was standing in the doorway of Laurel's room. By the way she was standing, I knew she was crying. I knew Laurel was right, too—she *was* stronger.

"She's gone, isn't she? That's where you went."

"I heard her go out the door. She was at the bus stop around the corner."

She nodded her head as if she knew from the beginning it would end this way.

"Did she explain it to you, Ben?" Her voice was tired. She stared into the empty room, waiting.

"She said she didn't know how to give love back."

She turned from the room and looked at me. There were still tears in her eyes.

"She tried, Ben."

"But not hard enough?"

"As best she could."

I waited for more, but she had turned again to face the empty room. The children were just beginning to stir in their beds. I thought, "Tiffany will be moving back into her room tonight." Ruth turned and put her arms around me without speaking.

"Ruth," I said, "why do we create for ourselves so much more pain than we were ever meant to endure? Why do we run from all that could bring us happiness?"

"Are you talking about Laurel?" she answered and then was silent.

I looked into the bedroom. The bed was made and spread on it were the new clothes, the shoes, the scriptures the missionaries had given her, and the art supplies. On top of the clothes was a sketch in soft pastels. I went in and picked it up. It was the pond with ducks swimming on the surface, wild flowers in the foreground, the Rockies lifting behind, and on the horizon two small doves flying into the pink and orange of an unseen sunset. The colors were perfect and everything was in balance.

# Chapter 13

The next days were hard on all of us. I suppose Ruth and I and even Brother Curtis expected Laurel to call or come back. Ruth didn't say much, but I knew she felt a deep sorrow. We passed the days with conflicting emotions. The third afternoon, Ruth and I couldn't stand it any longer.

"She would have gone back to Colfax for her other things, Ruth. Remember she said she wanted a place that nobody knew about. I know it's crazy, but couldn't we just drive down there? We don't have to get out of the car. We'll just drive and look."

We drove up and down Colfax for two hours. I was beginning to fight. The knots inside were pulling tighter with thoughts of an unborn baby and two people in California waiting to hear from LDS Social Services. It was hard to drive on Colfax, but I did so out of desperation. Ruth sat next to me the whole time, looking out the windows without speaking. Laurel was right; Ruth was stronger, she endured.

"She wanted to go to Estes Park," I remembered one evening. The next day we drove to Estes and spent the day walking around the shops and lake. In the stores we thought would appeal to Laurel, we described her to the owners. No one had seen her.

I spent hours walking Pearl Street one afternoon until it grew dark. She had once said she liked the street musicians, so I sat near them and searched the crowds. We spent two evenings at the art museum. Finally in gentleness, Ruth said, "You know what we're doing, Ben? We're refusing to let go, to accept."

"Do you accept it?"

"I have to. She made a choice. We have to let them make that choice. That's part of loving them, too."

I remembered Laurel's emotionless—almost casual—stare as she looked back at the house and at me in the window. "Okay, Ruth. Let's leave descriptions of her in all the places we can think of, then we'll stop and go back to a normal life."

A week later, we got a call one evening from the Denver Art Museum. They thought there was a girl matching Laurel's description, only she wasn't pregnant. We told them not to even approach her and tore out of the house. It was a thirty-minute drive. I prayed all the way down the freeway. We went to the front desk, but she had left fifteen minutes before we arrived.

"I thought I was getting over her," Ruth told me on the way home, then lapsed into silence. In the morning she called all the hospitals once again. There was no word. It was then we realized even if she had the baby, the hospital probably wouldn't call us. We thought we saw her everywhere, sleeping on a park bench, walking in the mall, looking at art supplies, or buying music in a music store. Everyone who was short and blonde pulled our heads in their direction, but each time the hope was in vain. Laurel was gone.

I don't know when the anger started again. Perhaps it was the need to explain Laurel's leaving, to find a scapegoat to lay our guilt and failure on. At some point during those days I felt a silence closing over my heart.

Where was the grateful acceptance of the good Samaritan, the peace of those on Christ's right hand? "Charity never faileth?" I said. But it did fail! The hatred and suffering caused it to fail.

"Couldn't You have stopped her, at least until the baby was born? Didn't that spirit deserve a chance to be born into a world of love and righteousness? We did all we could—and love drove her away. It wasn't supposed to fail. Where is the truth of the stories I've heard, and read, and spoken myself? Where are the endings I've believed in all my life? Where is she, Father? Where?"

I didn't get an answer. Four weeks later I heard on the news that a baby had been left, wrapped in blankets in a cardboard box, on the steps of the hospital in Estes Park. I knew it wasn't Laurel's. She could have never gone four weeks more, but I listened for the next two nights, as the whole state did, the unfolding story of a blonde, green-eyed baby girl the hospital nurses named April. No mother was ever found.

I'm not sure why I went up to Estes Park the next morning. It was foolish, and I didn't tell Ruth or Karen. I just cancelled my morning schedule, got in the car, and drove through the canyon and into Estes. When I got there, I asked directions to the hospital, then sat in the parking lot for half an hour, wanting to see Laurel come down the steps carrying the little girl they called April. I was still telling myself I was foolish as I walked up the steps, down the hallway to the maternity ward, and stopped in front of the glass partition that separated me from the newborn babies kicking or sleeping in the plastic covered domes, wrapped in their pink and blue blankets. There were three—two boys and a baby girl. The name at the end of her bed said "April" in bold pink letters.

I stared at her through the glass and thought of Laurel and knew again this wasn't her child, but I couldn't stop my tears from coming anyway. They came, and I wasn't ashamed of them, even when the nurse saw me standing by the window and came out to ask if she could help.

"No," I said, "I wish you could."

"Do you know about this child? I saw you staring at her."

"No. I have four children. They didn't come into the world this way."

She looked at me, then down to the baby. "What way?" she asked.

"Without love."

"Many come without love. That's not important. What's important is that they come. I felt like you the first time I saw her, too. Then I held her and bathed her, and it didn't matter anymore."

I stared through the separating glass, then looked at the nurse. It was such a relief to tell her. For twenty minutes I poured out my heart and Laurel's story to a woman whose name I read on her little white tag. She too was a stranger. It was fitting, for I never knew Laurel's real name. When I finished, she walked back into the nurse's station and brought out to me the familiar green hospital gown and fitted it over my shoulders and tied it at the back. Then she took me into the nursery and placed the tiny sleeping body of April into my arms and whispered, "Take as much time as you need."

I held her and moments later she awoke. I could feel the tiny head lying lightly in my palm, the pink blanket, soft and warm to my touch, smoothing the roughness of my hand. She moved and thrust a little fist in my direction, then arched her back and began to cry. I looked at the nurse. She smiled at me, then turned back to her work. I pulled the little body closer to me and felt the tiny warmth of life seeping through the blanket next to my heart. I thought of Laurel and love and life and cried long and hard and steadily while the nurse sat at her desk and waved everyone away, even the doctors.

I do not know when I stopped crying. I felt the nurse standing behind me and noticed the stillness. I looked down and April was quiet, staring into my face with eyes that could not yet focus, her tiny fist curled trustingly about my finger.

Then from that tiny, unwanted life that slept in innocence in my arms came His answer:

*That which you have done is not lost. Do you need an answer for your love? Is not the giving enough?*

I understood. A baby cried. I cried. They were all the answers I needed.

The little girl stirred in my arms, her tiny fingers clutched the edge of the blanket, then released it as I pulled her warmth against me once again. I remembered the little wistful song Laurel played over and over on the piano, a theme that now seemed tinged with hope, the hope that lives until the last petal falls.

# Epilogue

The story in the preceding pages is not just a story. With the exception of a few details, characters, and conversations, it happened as I have described it. I never meant to write it. It forced itself onto the page out of my struggle to comprehend why it ended the way it ended. Laurel and Adam came into our lives hurt and defeated, unable to pull together the pieces of their broken worlds. I wanted to help them with an urgency I had never experienced. They left, placing in my mind forever the shards of their worlds. I hurt and I fought, as I suspect those who read their story will hurt and fight. I could not understand why a boy who wanted forgiveness and peace could not find them; why a girl—a child really—who wanted forgetfulness and love ran from those aching to engulf her in the warmth and security of their love and understanding; why an unborn baby could not start life in the care of a young couple who had prayed for years to have a child.

In my life—perhaps it is true of yours as well—I had built up an expectation for happy endings, a belief, almost a demand, that love and service, desire and giving of self would always produce the positive rewards of change. If they did not, I had somehow failed and giving more love, giving more sacrifice would have produced the results I sought.

I went through a period of sullen anger where I could not pray about them because I knew, somehow, the answers I wanted Him to give me could not be given; that He would say, as He had said on other occasions of my life, "Be still and know that I am God." So I waited, forcing my prayers to race around the perimeters of my heart, hoping they would never slow enough to land upon the central concerns I knew were there. When the track became too worn to sustain the momentum there, God gave me His answer which slowly spiraled down till it hit the hollow of my heart: "Is not the giving enough?" I understood and accepted.

Laurel showed us a life without love, a life that was always victimized. We couldn't change it. We couldn't change Adam's, but they let us rise above ourselves and love and sacrifice and feel deeply.

I cannot say that I have resolved all the emotions and questions Laurel and Adam brought me. Nor did the writing of their stories settle the memories to more comfortable positions in my mind. However, I learned much about the suffering of innocence and the suffering of guilt. Perhaps these two agonies are not too distant from each other. I learned in the tiniest, minute degree the weight of the glory of God and I learned that giving, no matter the result, must always be its own answer. It must always be enough. Perhaps the most difficult lesson in life is to accept that answer without cynicism or despair or any hesitancy to give more.

—S. Michael Wilcox